MW00942867

KARL J. JUNES

Karl J. Junes

Copyrighted © 2018 by Karl J. Junes

All Rights Reserved

CONTENT

<u>SPECIAL THANKS TOO</u>

Lurnas-Tumblr
(Character Designing)

Gummy Doodles-Tumblr
(Character designing)

ALBA RMZ-Art Station
(Cover creator)

My Auntie

My Mom

My Dad

Prologue

A Universe. Pretty big? Am I right? It's HUGE!, But you don't (actually) know how big a universe is. Not sure if I could ever tell how big it could actually be, since it's always expanding every single second, so it's always getting bigger and bigger and bigger. Seems endless. Something has to fill all of this space, and not just let it sit there, and collecting dust. Well, not dust, really, just sitting there.

Have you ever wondered, is it really just us? Here, alone in the black empty void of space. Only our home planet seems to have life, but the nine other planets (counting Pluto) have no life whatsoever. Everything is created for a reason, so why hasn't there been any other life? Scientists every year seemed to discover new galaxies full of planets. Yet, no (other) life has ever been discovered. They found water on Mars, but no life.

Planets and planets, galaxies and galaxies, and I'm saying again, no life.

Well, I don't think I could tell you that there is life out there, but what if I told you that there *is* a galaxy. Lightyears and lightyears away from our own galaxy. In a galaxy far, far away, but maybe not so long ago.

But simply, another galaxy. A galaxy that is full of life! Imagine that there's a galaxy full of planets, and each planet has their very own life-form. Eleven planets in this galaxy to be exact. There's a planet full of rock people, another one full of fire people, water people, plant people, magical people, robot people, sky people, sound people, and animal people.

Each one blooming with life, and living in ways we don't usually live. The people in this galaxy are very different than us. Very different. They're called Kausnian's, the beings in this universe.

There is one planet that where all of these beings all come together. They all get along, no matter how different (they are) from one another. Doesn't matter if someone has brown, blue or purple skin. Furry, scaly, or metal skin, it doesn't matter what you look like, or who you are. Everyone is treated the same. They treat others how they wanted to be treated.

A planet where everything is literally possible. You wanna look for a unicorn, you could. You wanna fly with dragons, you could! Could go treasure hunting and sail the seas. Or just chill and eat bamboo with pandas.

This planet is bigger than the sun. Maybe even five time bigger than it.

This planet is named....

Seighdarr

(Say-duh-are)

Chapter 01:
Adventure

Space, it's *so* pretty. You could take a look by stepping outside of your house, looking out the window, or looking up an image on the internet. Images of space are magnificent. Colourful too, and filled with quintillions and quintillions of stars, galaxies, planets, and universes. Who knows how big the universe is, or if there is ever an ending to space. From research, folks say that the universe is always growing about sixty-seven kilometers per second. The Pinwheel galaxy is where this story begins. Near a planet that is five times the size of our sun. It has seven colourful rings circling the planet, and is all six of the primary and secondary colours, and white rings circling them. Around the planet, there are a total of ninety-seven moons, so no matter when you look up into the sky during the day or night, you'll always be able to have a sight of the moons of a beautiful colour.

Flying past the rings, and coming into orbit of the planet is a medium- sized, blue spaceship with white designing on the top and sides. On both sides of this medium ship said "*Hyper Nova*," in a big red font. Coming in from space, which is normal for this planet where space ships come into the planet's orbit all the time, the ship had it courses set on forest-y grasslands. Filled with tall and wavy grass, slow flowing rivers, animals of all types, and a small farming town in the middle of all of it. The ship was cruising through the skies, which were very calm and peaceful , like everything else all around.

Flying in closer and closer from space, and nearing the ground, it landed near the small farming town. Air decompressed from pipes all around the skip, lights flickering and spinning, four landing wheels legs folded out from the bottom of the corners . Landing a mile away from the town, and it hid in the forest of, what seemed to be, cottonwood trees. The ship slowly hovered closer and closer , when it finally touched down on the wild grass. Air whooshing from exhaust vents, the two jet engines winding down, lights flickered off, and the ship had completely turned off within a few minutes. Back of the ship is a large rectangular door was folded into the ship. Caution lights began to flicker, air compressed out from the door, and folding out of the ship, a cargo bay was revealed behind that door. The door touching the grass and extra weights extending from the sides, finally resting. The ship finally winding down and cooled off.

A figure appeared from within the ship, and it stepped forward and walked through the cargo door, then stood in the sunlight . Coming out of the ship, it appeared to be a blue skin-coloured girl with short royal blue hair and royal blue eyes. Wearing a white, black and blue body suit and holding space headgear in her right arm. Her left hand resting on her hip. She stood there proud, and took in a deep breath through her nose, and breathing it out through her mouth.

"Haaaaa...." She sighed. Staring off into the tops of the trees, and feeling as she is at peace when seeing the green leaves of the tree wave in the wind. "Well, you did it, Avonlea. You made it to your new home," she smiled. She just felt the cool breeze being blown against her face, and through her hair. She turned around, and walked back into her ship.

Later on, Avonlea had gone back into her ship and gotten a new outfit. She steps out of her ship, and onto the cargo door where it was angling downward. Avonlea had put on her normal and casual outfit. A bright red tank top with royal blue trimming. Dark blue sport shorts with lime green lining on the sides and bright purple trimming at the bottom. Dark blue gloves with bright purple circle on the top of her hand. Bright red sneakers with dark blue laces and white soles. She also wore a dark blue necklace, and bright yellow goggles with orange lenses. Also, on her shoulders, she has tattoos. On her right is a simple star, and a gear on her right with a star in the middle. With her, she had a fabric purple pocketbook. In it, she had a bunch of personal info she had to carry around with her, and her currency of comet coins. She also packed a large coin that's five inches wide with a star logo on the front. Before placing it in her pocket, she glanced at it for a second.

"Hm, you never know," she said as she stares at it. She slips it into her pocket separately. Her pocketbook on her right pocket and the coin on her left. Stepping off the lowered cargo door, she stepped onto the tall and wild grass surrounding her ship. She felt it brush against her lower legs. Laughing for a bit as it tickled her. She took another step into a bald spot in the grass. Moist soil beneath her shoe sank in. Going over it, she lifted her shoe and bits of grass and soil stuck to the bottom.

Gazing around at the familiar sights , but never appreciated how wonderful it all is. Coming in closer to one of the cottonwood trees that are present all around her, she saw a trail of ants marching along the side. Placing her hand against it she felt the rough bark. Taking her hand away from the tree, she viewed her palm to see bits of bark and dirt that had come off onto her hand. As she was walking, she felt the lumpy ground and how uneven it was with each step she took. Her right foot would be higher, her left lower, or it would be the other way around. When looking up into the heads of the twisted branches of the trees, the sunlight of the white suns would beam in her face. Then she would see those eye floaters.

"Gosh dang it!" She said. No matter where she looked, those floaters would always be there. As we know, they eventually go away. Continuing to go in the same direction, she came across a fallen cottonwood tree with moss growing along the side of it. She stretched her left leg over the log, and placed both legs on the other side. As she's taking her stroll through the forest, she would see small cotton bits fall from the trees. Some would fall in her hair without knowing, and some on her clothes. Still she was unaware.

Going along the path she spotted in the distance, the small town she landed nearby . Walking towards the grey asphalt road that's in a ninety- degree angle, An angle faced away from her. Just next to it is a man- built canal with concrete walls along the sides of the road. When she approached the canal there didn't seem to be a. way over the canal, and just the streaming water. Avonlea backed up from the canal and charged to hop over the water. Landing on the other side, she gazed around her. It wasn't what she expected when looking around.

"Wow, this is a lot different than....well...home. No rushing engines everywhere, and people," she said. Walking towards the first building, a small food store. Nothing that she hasn't seen, but the people in the small town are really strange. Coming out of the store, from Avonlea's view was a normal- looking girl with short blonde hair, purple skin, and in a green dress, seemed pretty normal. But on the top of her head were two long bunny ears. One being straight up, and one being floppy. Avonlea stared at them, and was sure they were fake when approaching her. That's when the girl raised her bunny ears up and down, then walked away from the store.

"Whoa. They said they'd be different people on this planet. This is what they were talking about," she told herself. Near the entrance of the store, another one of those beings came walking out of the store. This time, it was a boy with black hair, brown skin, green eyes, but he had a long fluffy tail, black cat ears, and whiskers. When he stepped out, he yawned, showing his canine teeth. Then he walked away from the store. Avonlea just stared at him, and noticed there were other people just like the bunny girl and cat boy.

"Okay, okay, okay, a new race of people, it's fine. It's normal to everyone here, so I'll go with it," she said. Another person with green lizardskin came walking out with a bagful of chips. "Yeah. Completely normal." She did see some normal- looking folks. That she could tell. A person with royal blue skin, and bright yellow hair flew away from a store just down the street. Walking past the small food store and over to some others down the street, on the left while walking down the sidewalk she notices a magic shop, on the right is a hardware store, but in the alleyway of that hardware store

- 17 -

there was some scrap. "Now I know where to go for parts," she said
to herself.

Going further down the sidewalk, she passed by Kausnian's
and the other animal people she ran into. Hover vehicles would pass
by her. . No other buildings were around this next corner that Avonlea went around, and was next to the side of the magic shop she just
passed by. "Huh, this place seems pretty cool——" then she fell.
"AH!" She shouted. She looked to what she landed on, and she had
landed upon a person. She looked, and the person was looking right
at her. "Oh, my stars," she said, and quickly got up, "My bad, I wasn't
watching where I was going." She appeared to have fallen upon a girl
a lot shorter than her. The girl had literal snow- white skin, short
royal blue hair and eyes. A royal blue pro shirt and black sport shorts.
A white headband, knee high blue and white shoes and royal blue
bracelets.

"Are you alright?" Said Avonlea. The girl sat there on the
concrete ground, staring back at Avonlea as she stood up.

"I am terrific. How are you?" Said the girl.

"Uh, I'm great," said Avonlea in a cheerful way. Avonlea held
out a hand. The girl held her hand, and Avonlea pulled her up. She
was much shorter than Avonlea as Avonlea stood in front of her. As
Avonlea viewed the girl more, the more she seemed strange.

"My name is NASIA. It's a joy to meet someone entirely
new," said NASIA.

"Oh, hello, it's nice to meet you too. I'm Avonlea."

"I-I-I-I-I-I haven't seen you around in t-t-t-town before. So,
you m-must be n-new," said NASIA.

"You feeling alight? Your head isn't hurting from the concrete?" Said Avonlea.

"I am terribly sorry. I recently have installed a brand- new
processor-27 and a new routing system. Still proc-c-c-cessing the
error-r-r-rs." Avonlea was confused.

"Processor? What are talking about——are you sure I didn't
hit your head hard on the concrete?"

"Possibly. I'll have to have a check- up with my designer just
in case?" Avonlea still being confused.

"Um. Alright, whatever you..." suddenly, just in the distance
behind Avonlea, there was a sudden **boom!** Avonlea froze and so did
NASIA.

"What was that?"

"Hmm, not sure?" said NASIA.

"What am I doing just standing here!?" Said Avonlea. Avonlea quickly turned around, and ran as quickly as she could down the
sidewalk. Going down the street, from where she and NASIA had
been talking, smoke and debris flew everywhere. By blowing some of
it away, and she tried to get a clear view of what was going on. That's
when a large stone came flying at her! She jumped back, and it barely
skimmed over her back, and rolled over to the sidewalk. A large
shadowy figure appeared in the dust, and jumped out!

"No simple jail can hold me!" A woman's voice came from
the dust. That's when a massive woman stepped out from the dust-
cloud. She seemed well over six feet. Tall than Avonlea. She had short
dark purple hair, bright hot pink skin. Her biceps were both glowing
a red light, and her forearms glowed a bright orange. Maybe it was
super powers, but her arms got a little bigger, and now had an armor

around them. With that, the woman swung both arms into the air and jumped. Landing back down with an all mighty swing from the sky and crashing down in the middle of the road. Cracking the road, and making buildings along with roads uneven. People tumbled and windows shattered, the woman got up, and laughed with all of her might!

"TORA STANDS BENEATH YOU!" The woman shouted. People ran, and she appeared to have busted out of the jail that's nearby . Three police women came running out of the hole she had made, and chased after her. The police on this planet don't wear the same uniform as we all know. They do have the blue, red and white on them still, but they all have an armor suit with police lights flashing on their shoulders. The word police on their upper back. Also, it's equipped with a load of gadgets. An officer in her mid- thirty's name of Officer Barron came running after Tora.

"Stop! Put your hands in the air!" said Officer Barron. Tora turned around and swung her fist at her to send her flying back into the hole of the police station. She did the same with the other two officers that came walking up toward Tora.

"Anyone else here to challenge me!?" Said Tora. Avonlea ran to the side of a building where no-one could see her. She pulled out that coin from her left pocket and raised it up to her face.

"I knew I would need this. Suit up!" With a press of a button on that coin, Avonlea placed it on her chest where the star logo lit up. The coin then sent a blue light outline all over Avonlea's body, except for her head. The coin appeared to be a full body suit that was able to build around Avonlea's body. After it formed around her, it lit up with a cyan light outline . Her outfit is mainly white and dark

blue with the star logo glowing on her chest, and the name "AVON-
LEA" on her chest .

    "Oh yeah! Astronaut Avonlea ready to protect and serve!"
She said, and checked herself out before going to face Tora. "Let's
bring it on!" She shouted, and she ran out of that alleyway , to find
Tora following a road that lead out of town, but that's when Avonlea
stood in the middle of the road when no-one else would.

    Standing in the road with both fists on her hips.

    "STOP!" she shouted. Tora stopped in her tracks to look
back at the smiling being. "Look, if we could go straight to you going
back to jail, it would be awesome," said Avonlea.

    "Ha-ha-ha-haa! What jail or prison could contain me?! With
all of this power?! Naw, man. I have big plans for the future! Letting
some little girl get in my way is the same as an ant getting in my——"
Avonlea has a spectacular super power. Avonlea is a shapeshifter.
Her whole body is made up of one-quintillion micro cubes that are
able to change into any object that she can think of. She transformed
her forearm into grappling hooks, and attached them to both of
Tora's forearms. Avonlea pulled and tried to get her to go back to jail.

    "Sorry. You'll have to wait your time in jail, buddy, but for
now, you're coming with me!" said Avonlea, and with all of her
strength, she began to pull against Tora, who was not even moving a
centimeter.

    "Oh, no, the little blue girl got...." Tora with her super
strength pulled Avonlea towards her very quickly, which Avonlea
expected Tora gave Avonlea some momentum to fly at her. Avonlea
came at her, legs first, she turned them into a hard metal wall, and
BASHED against Tora. Sending Tora to the ground. Tora quickly got

up, picked up Avonlea by the right bicep, but Avonlea climbed to her back, and turned her forearms into jackhammers to pound against Tora's back. Then she smacked her head. Tora reached over her back and grabbed her right bicep again to pull her over her shoulder, and threw her against the asphalt ground.

"YOU ARE NOTHING!!" said Tora. Tora had her right- hand gripping Avonlea's neck. Avonlea quickly acted by attaching a silver bracelet to Tora's right wrist, and to her left, from her bodysuit. Magnetic cuffs that quickly activated. Forcing Tora's wrists to attach to each other. Avonlea jumped away as Tora tried to pull her wrists apart, but couldn't. Avonlea went behind her, and attached a metal clamp to her ankle that stuck to the asphalt, so she wasn't able to get up at all. Avonlea ran in front of Tora with a smirk on her face.

"Hah! Even the smallest ants can get in the way of a massive chugging train. Aye? Bud?" said Avonlea. Before Tora could say any-thing, the police walked behind her with laser blasters, and other equipment.

"Hands up! Blue girl!" said Officer Barron. Avonlea did raise her arms, and turned around.

"Aw, come on! I did you job for——" before she could finish her sentence, Avonlea turned her right forearm into a grappling hook again and latched onto the ground to pull herself away from the po-lice.

"STOP!" shouted Officer Barron, and the Police ran after Avonlea, circling around Tora as well, beginning to take her back to jail. Another ability that Avonlea possesses is the power of super speed, so she quickly ran for forest hill sides, and ran and ran deep within it. She ran behind a big cottonwood tree that was bigger than

the others, and looked around to be sure she wasn't followed. Luckily, she wasn't.

"Phew!" said Avonlea. By pressing another button on the star
shape on her chest, the whole- bodysuit all went back into the coin,
and caught it before it dropped off of her. "Wow. My first save. I feel
great! Hm? Maybe a run in the forest behind this place? Maybe I
could lay low for a bit?" After thinking it over, Avonlea placed her
coin back into her left pocket, and sprinted away into the forest, and
over the hills.

Chapter 02: Aspect

Zooming through the forest, and beyond those hills, she was already having a great time. With her super speed, Avonlea is able to view the forest from left to right. If she was approaching a tree as a fast pace, she won't stop, but would quickly veer left. That also goes for if she comes across a dead end. Speeding through the forest, left, right, she saw cottonwood trees, some being as tall as a five- story building, or as small as a dog house. They were all spread out, too. In between the trees are spots of open grass plains.

Avonlea jumped over a large hole, and landed on the other side where a fallen tree hung over her direction. She slid on her back where she turned into a tire, rolled on the ground, jumped from her tire form and kept running. Large mushrooms were up ahead. She hopped straight into the air and bounced off the mushroom, which in turn released a noxious odor, and luckily, she wasn't around to take it in. Coming to a dead end where a bunch of bush shrubs were . Quickly turning left and going into a different direction. A straight runway of grass plain was upon her, so with all the energy she had, she ran as fast as she could down the pathway of grass. Suddenly and slowly, a herd of triceratops slowly came walking onto the path. Avonlea quickly acted by sliding on her back again, missing the foot nearly pressing against her, but made it out okay to keep running.

I should mention that dinosaurs do exist on the planet of Seighdarr, and they also possess some different abilities and come in different varieties. Like, triceratops can come in the normal version of themselves, or come with a gemstone like skin, or metal skin, almost resembling a robot.

Avonlea kept running and running. The adrenaline rushed through her veins, the sweat flying from her forehead, and her heart pumping. Heavy breathing, she loved it. Running past a tree arch to where she found different species of trees.. The trees around her seemed to be jackal berry trees. Large quantities of them all bunched up around her.. Avonlea stopped to take in the view of the trees before her. She took in a deep breath through her nose, and let it out through her mouth while she closed her eyes.

"Oh my gosh, I've been waiting since...well....FOREVER to feel this again. The cool breeze, the sunshine on my ugly vucting face. Grass is not cyan, but whatever." Avonlea spread her arms, and fell on her back and onto the tall and wild grass. "AAAHHHHhhh..." she felt relieved, and closed her eyes, rested both palms behind her head and laid her right leg over her left.

"ow!" A faint voice shouted in the distance. Avonlea opened her eyes, and turned her head to the left. Squinting her eyes to think.

"Did I just hear a voice?" She said. Still laying on the ground, she sat up to be sure she did hear what she heard.

"ow!" Again, she heard.

"Uh-oh. Someone's hurting." She quickly got up, and sprinted towards the direction she had heard it coming from. She ran up to a spot near a clutter of the jackal berry trees to scan her area. It was then when she spotted a flipped over wheelchair, and someone on the ground. "Uh-oh," she said. She quickly ran over to the person, and when she got closer to the person, it seemed to be a girl. She had a cool hair cut where half of her head, the left side is shaven dark red hair, but also had a design of stars. Light brown skin, bright red eyes. On the right side is bright red short hair that was a gradient between red and yellow with the mix of orange in the middle. She wore two tank tops with thin shoulder straps. The inner one is dark pink, and the outer one a dark grey. She wore dark blue jeans with rips in the knees, a dark pink belt and dark knee- high pink boots. Avonlea walked over to her, picked her up.

"Whoa!" Said the girl, "What's happening? What's going on? Who's touching me? Tengo poderes de fuego," she said. Avonlea held the girl in her arms, and with one foot was able to flip over the girl's wheel chair, and place her back into it. .

"Phew. Relax, I'm just...."

"Back off, I can do this myself," said the girl in anger, and her head literally caught fire.

"Woah, woah, woah! No need of a tan, bud, I saw someone off their wheel chair toppled over, I came to help. Like, who wouldn't help someone to their chair?" She didn't say anything, but turned away while giving her a very snarky look while slowly rolling away.

"Hey, I'm sorry you could have done it yourself, but I can't just.....leave someone there in need!" Said Avonlea. The girl stopped, and turned slightly towards her.

"Eh. It's fine, or whatever," she said, and the fire went out. Avonlea walked along with her as she began to roll.

"Are you one of those people who are wheelchair bound, and hate being helped because you feel useless?" The girl stopped, and slightly turned towards her. She looked at Avonlea, then away at another direction, then back at her.

"Yeah." The girl looked at Avonlea from head to foot. "How could you know that?"

"Well, let's say that I know someone that lost her leg, an arm and an eye. I helped her with everyday things, such as writing, getting somewhere she needed, and simple things like getting her food. After a while, she hated it all because she felt like she wasn't able to do anything anymore. From then on, I let her do things her own, but she did need my help from time to time. I think she figured out I was only trying to help."

"It's just...It's not like I don't want the help, I just don't need it every day. I can care for myself. I can fly! I have my fire! Radar bison. Just because I'm wheelchair bound and blind, doesn't make me useless."

"Oh, I didn't even know you're blind. GEEZ, and you made it all the way out here?! You're like five miles away from town! What a champ, dude."

"Hah. Thanks. You know, you're the first person to understand that. Thanks, and sorry."

"Eh, it's alright. But if you're blind, how do you know you're looking at me? Is it my voice, or sound direction? You're blind, but have that small bit of sight?" asked Avonlea.

"Uh, no. I have radar vision. If this makes sense, but I can see the outlines of people and other things. Like I can see the outline of you, but——"

"OH! You can see the outline of me, but not what my face looks like. I get it."

"Yeah," the girl began rolling in her direction.

"You said I'm five miles away from town? Where are you from?"

"Uh....I don't know what the town is called. Flip, but it had a small food store, magic shop and a hardware store with a bunch of scrap around it."

"Oh, yeah you're talking about...my home town, Farmington. And I clearly went in the wrong direction."

"Where you heading? Oh, wait, my name is Avonlea Jyuinz. So, I'm not mysterious to you."

"Avonlea, huh? Sup, dude. Colomar Junlo. There's a spot near Farmington, uh...I want to go to," said Colomar. While talking, they began to go in the same direction together. Avonlea following Colomar into a bunch of jackal berry trees. To where it was very shaded from the sun.

Colomar is able to roll over the grass with ease in her wheel chair. She kept up with Avonlea at a normal walking speed.

"So, where's the town ?" Asked Colomar.

"Uh...." With Avonlea having super speed, she had strong legs, so she super jumped as high as she could to see the town just over the hills.

"Yeah, we're about four and a half miles away from the town. I'm laying low for a bit, now."

"Did you steal a cabbage, too?" Said Colomar

"Uh.....no." said Avonlea.

"Nnnnneither did I."

"Someone broke out of jail, I beat her up for a bit and made the police mad, somehow and I'm just going to lay low."

"Ppppfff. I say, just whatever, "I did your job when you didn't", said Colomar.

"Someone named Tora? Broke out."

"Hm. Don't know her." Walking through a shadowy part of the trees, Avonlea and Colomar went around a rock formation that stuck up from the ground. They weren't aware that there was a red string placed beneath the roots of the grass they walked on. Letting something know of their presence. Not with Colomar, but with Avonlea is when she walked through some very tall grass, and beneath the grass was the red string sticking to the bottom of her shoe. Suddenly, a big SNAP occurred, and following it were big thumping noises. Avonlea kept walking, but listened for the noise again. Colomar stopped when she saw Avonlea peering around her.

"What?" Said Colomar.

"Did you hear that?" Said Avonlea.

"No. What was it?" Avonlea standing three feet away from Colomar in front of her, turned away from her.

"That thumping noise. I heard something. It sounded like running."

"So? Any animal could be running around here." Avonlea turned around.

"I mean, the..." that's when she turned around, to find right behind Colomar are eight thin legs standing behind Colomar, and attached to the legs is a creature with large red fangs, and eight beady eyes ready to bite into Colomar.

"WOOOOOOOAAAAAAHHHHH!!!!" Screamed Avonlea, and she picked Colomar out from her wheelchair, and the creature with the legs immediately destroyed her wheelchair. Avonlea, holding Colomar in her arms, turned her right arm into a blaster to fire at the creature, who appeared to be a spider. With slender black and red legs that were attached to the creature's upper and lower back. Each one of the legs also had claws the size of a car tire. . Four eyes in the front, two on the side and two more on the back. With none of them blinking or moving around. The spider wore a black body suit, with a black and red trench coat, black and red jeans and black boots. Black gloves and wore a mask that cover their spider whole face, except the eyes. Also wearing a long brimmed black hat.

Avonlea jumped back, and up to the top of a hill, and pointed her blaster at the spider creature .

"Hey, what's going on?! What are you doing?" Said Colomar

"I know you don't see! But do you see the outline of that spider creature?!" Said Avonlea. Colomar looked. At the outline where she pointed her blaster, and standing where Colomar looked stood the spider creature. The spider creature stood incredibly still (and stared) at them.

"I think, I see him?" Said Colomar. That's when the spider creature shot them with some bright red webs, and shot them at Colomar's leg.

"ARGH!" She said. Suddenly, the spider person sent a surge of red electricity down the webs, and electrocuted the both of them.

"WAH WHA WHA HAW REEEYYAAAAWWW!!!!" They both shouted as the electricity crossed over from Colomar to Avonlea. Avonlea fell over and dropped Colomar. Colomar passed out from the electricity, and the spider creature began to pull her (to them) with the webs still attached to her. Avonlea quickly grabbed on her arm, and pulled! The spider creature, being very strong pulled hard, too. Avonlea turned her arm into a long sword to cut the web, and held onto Colomar to roll down the hill on the other side. When coming to the bottom, Colomar was still passed out. Stopping next to a tree, Avonlea laid Colomar on her back.

"Hey, Colomar, wake up. Are you alright?" Avonlea smacked her face lightly. She began slightly to awaken.

"Hu? Augh.....wa...?" said Colomar. Suddenly, Avonlea was shot in the back with the web, was drawn back over the hill, and was slammed face first into the ground! Avonlea looked up to see the slender legs crawling towards her, and the spider creature spun more webs from the heels of their legs. Picking up Avonlea, they wrapped up Avonlea in a red web to look like a burrito. Nothing but her head was sticking out. The spider creature came walking up, and picked up Avonlea to hold her next to its face.

"Alright, spider. What you going to do? Eat me?" said Avonlea.

"Consume. Hunt," spidertook off its mask, and showed its mouth, wide open. Touching both sides of its ears, razor sharp teeth growing bigger, and had two large red fangs. "The Art....of Vyroz." With the black beady eyes, spider looked at Avonlea with all four of its front eyes. Vyroz's mouth grew bigger, and leaned in toward Avonlea's face.

"Well, I had a good run," said Avonlea. That's when fire was blasted at Vyroz. Vyroz turns and screams into the direction of the fire where Colomar was flying with her eyes, hair and palms in flames.

"Feel the flames. Touch me, and you'll burn!" Said Colomar. Colomar threw a fire ball at Vyroz. It burned the webs Avonlea was wrapped in, and she kicked Vyroz in the face to quickly jump away. Avonlea turned her arms into blasters to shoot Vyroz. The fire and blaster lasers didn't affect Vyroz, but it burned. So Vyroz hissed, and put on its mask to quickly vanish from their sight.

Avonlea changed her arms back into -normal and quickly ran back towards Colomar up on the hill.

"Thanks, Colomar, but we gotta go!" said Avonlea.

"I think we can take that thing on!" said Colomar. Avonlea jumped to catch her wrist and dragged her down on the ground to start running to town.

"Hey! Let go! I can handle this!" She said. Avonlea zoomed back in the direction on where the town was at.

"It's not that I think you can't do it, it's that I don't think both of us can do it. I hate to run away from a fight, Colomar, but I'm not dying from some spider!" Said Avonlea.

"True," said Colomar, and flew with her back to the hill near the town.

Much later, the both made it to the edge of town. Standing on the hills next to the town where it was covered by trees, Avonlea and Colomar sat next to a large cottonwood tree, with Avonlea very exhausted.

Heavy breathing "Ugh. That….was stupid," said Avonlea. Colomar had her back against the tree.

"Yeah. Uh…you going to be okay?" asked Colomar, who was just fine.

"Yeah, I'm fine….when."

"I saw you shoot that thing. You have a blaster?"

"No. It's from my.....phew....super power. I'm a.....shapeshifter. I can turn any part....uh....of my body into things. Like a blaster....but the laser blasts takes a lot of my energy. And we just ran back over here in five minutes, so...yeah...I think I'm going to be alright," said Avonlea.

"Shapeshifter? That's awesome! Although, I can't see what you could turn into." Avonlea stood up.

"OH!!! Woah! Okay. I got my energy back. Sorry we couldn't get to where you wanted to go, and your wheel chair was destroyed."

"Eh, it's fine. I didn't need it for much longer, anyways. But, let's go to where I wanna chill ," said Colomar. Colomar flew up into the air, and looked around. Her sight could be difficult for her sometimes with people and different objects looking the same. But one spot near this town, she knew quite well.

"This way!" She said, and quickly took off. Avonlea saw her fly towards a hill.

"Ugh....alright," said Avonlea. She took off, and chased her. Quickly, they were getting to their destination where there a tall hill with one cottonwood tree was , and she saw Colomar sitting up on the top. Avonlea raced to the back of it, and ran up the steep incline.

"HAUGH! HAUGH! HAUGH! HAUGH!" She groaned as she climbed up the hill, and fell to her knees when getting to the top, climbing on her knees to find Colomar laying on her stomach and looking over the edge.

"Augh! Came up here? To lay on the hill?" huffed Avonlea. Avonlea crawled next to Colomar.

"No. I.....lay up here, sometimes I lay up here to see the out-lines of the town. I just.....try to imagine what It would look like. Tell anyone this, I'll burn you!" Said Colomar, and lit her hand on fire.

"Hah. I'll tell everyone, everyone in the whole world." Colo-mar laughs.

Avonlea laid on her stomach and laid next to Colomar.

"What did you mean when you didn't need your wheelchair? Are you going to just fly?"

"No. Tomorrow, I'm getting leg enhancers. I forgot what my condition was called with my legs, but my leg muscle didn't develop right, but with the enhancers, I'm able to walk normally. They're like metal leggings attached to the side of my legs."

"That's good. Really good. How long have you been like this, though?"

"Well, I was born like this, and have never been able to see. They do tell me that blue is cold and red is hot. They tell me water is blue, fire is red, sky is blue and clouds are white. For my legs, it be-gan when I was little. I had an accident in a tree where I fell, and it messed up my leg development or something. It's coming back, like really slow. By the time I'm thirty years old, I'll be able to naturally walk again."

"That's also really...."

"I don't know why people see or know that I'm blind or in a wheel chair, they always assume that I'm helpless. I'm helpless! I'm the opposite! I live on my own, and I'm able to do a hand stand."

"I know, I know. If that one moment of me helping made you mad, I'm sorry."

"It's alright. I'm just kind of tired of it, is all."

"Ever wish to see?"

"No. Vuct that. I love that everything is a mystery to me. If I was born like this, it means it has a purpose behind it. So, I'd rather stay blind. I make jokes about me being in a wheel chair and being blind. Like EVIL nemesis is CHAIR!" Said Colomar. Avonlea laughed!

"Ha-ha-ha-ha, or my stars," said Avonlea.

"Hah-hah! One time, when I was sixteen, I stayed at a hotel for an event I was going to, and when I went to it, I got the top story, and the lady was all like, "Great, choice, ma'am, your room has a GREAT view!" And I was like, "Ohhohh, thanks...."

"Oh, my stars," laughed Avonlea.

"So, go full out with the jokes. I especially like the blind jokes. I can never see them coming," Colomar laughed.

"Oh my....CHEESE! It's what call the CHEESY JOKES!" Said Avonlea.

"Okay-okay, I got another one. I do think of becoming a stand- up comedian, but I'm not sure if they'll roll with it?"

"Oh, my stars, stop!" Avonlea laughed.

"Hah-hah, I can't take that joke. I remember hearing that from a talent TV show," said Colomar.

"Oh....my stars, it's good. You know, some people like you, and I'm referring to you being blind or being in a wheelchair, some people make fun of that fact that they have disabilities."

"I learned that long time ago. I woke up one day and realized if I kept telling myself I'm helpless in that chair, I can't accomplish anything."

"Yeah! Someone once told me, people don't have disabilities, they just do things their own way," said Avonlea.

"Yeah! man! Although, I do remember falling down the stairs in my wheel chair, and my chair landed perfectly with me, and I landed back in my wheel chair perfectly, too! It vucting hurt, though."

"I bet," said Avonlea. "You know, I just moved here to this small town to start fresh, and you're the coolest girl I've ever met in my life," said Avonlea.

"Hah, never heard that in my life. Thanks. Where did you come from?" Said Colomar.

"I'm from.....Solvar."

"Cool."

"What do you do these days, though? What do you want in your life?" Asked Avonlea.

"Well. I......hm....I sound weird, but I've been wanting, forever to become an author of books." Colomar looks over to Avonlea, and she doesn't see her face, but the outline of it looking at her.

"Huh?"

"Strange right?!"

"No. I've heard stranger, but how can you reach that?"

"I don't know. I can't write or type. I tried an audio book, but I couldn't."

"Couldn't you tell someone to type your idea? Maybe that could start?"

"Yeah. It's a fiction book, and my ideas are kind off...weird. I always thought of making music, and music is the only thing in the WORLD that means a lot to me!" said Colomar.

"Oh. 'Cause you can't see, and all?" said Avonlea. Colomar slowly turns her head to Avonlea, and wasn't sure if she was looking straight at Avonlea, but Avonlea saw the strange look on her face.

"No, man, it's just...I love how the album cover art looks...... OF COURSE IT'S THE MUSIC!!!" She burst, and Avonlea burst into laughter.

"Hah-hah! I know, I'm sorry. I had that one floating in my head the moment you said I could make blind jokes and the mention of music."

"Oh...hah hah. My jokes be the bomb."

"Be the bomb? More like be the cheese."

"Whatever."

The two of them seemed to chat for hours and hours on top of that hill. Until the dawn of light began to show at the horizon of the other hills.

"You know, I like you. You're pretty cool, dude," said Colomar

"Thanks. You too. Makes us friends, then?" said Avonlea. Avonlea held out a fist, and made sure she was able to see it.

Colomar made a fist, and they both fist- bumped.

" Definite friends, Avonlea."

Chapter 03:
The Gift

Nightfall had arrived, and Avonlea walked with Colomar , as she flew to her home. Having a nice conversation about whatever came to mind, and nonsensical stuff like movies they've seen, music they listen to, and food they eat. Not far from the town that is called Farmington. Just over a couple of hills and near cottonwood tree that is bigger than they usually grow to is a box- shaped home that sits right next to a tree. It's made of a dark wood with big open windows, and having two stories. A gravel trail was all that lead to Colomar's home, and they both followed it. Coming up to the front porch, Avonlea was again talking with Colomar.

"...and dude, you have a nice house! Where did you get it?" said Avonlea.

"I had it build for me from my family. Made just for me, and stuff inside is specifically for me." Colomar only saw the outlines of most things of her house. Her front porch had nothing on it, but as they came back, she noticed a box that was half the size of the front door.

"Oh, my stars!" She said, and quickly flew towards it. Hovering next to it, she felt it. "Oh, my stars! What does it say on the box!" said Colomar. Avonlea saw the excited look on her face. She walked onto the porch, and saw a large white box, and vertically on the box, it said....

"Uh....it says "5132, Colomar Junlo, Farmington, FR, AIRA" in big bold..." Colomar gasped in and picked up, flew too quickly and not knowing where the door was at and flew into the wall. Felt around for the door handle, turned the handle to quickly flew inside her house. Avonlea followed her, and closed the door behind. Stepping onto a bright red carpet and onto smooth wooden floors, Colomar shouted "Take off your shoes!" Avonlea took them off with the laces still tied and had her white and red sox touch the wooden floor. Literally sliding around. Colomar brought the box to th counter top in her kitchen, and flew around.

"Knife! Knife! Where's a knife!?" shouted Colomar. Avonlea walked over, and with her index and middle finger she formed a knife. She slid her knife fingers across and cut the tape as she did.

"Don't worry, I got you covered." The box had two flaps, so she crossed her knife finger on the sides and in the middle. Finally opened up, Avonlea opened the cardboard box. Colomar took out another box, but it's an alloy blue colour with the name "AIRA" on top. She pushed the cardboard box aside, and she placed the alloy box on the counter top.

"Avonlea! Follow me!" Said Colomar, and flew up a set of stairs. Avonlea quickly followed her up the stairs. Colomar quickly went though some of her drawers by a nightstand next to her bed. Colomar sat down, and took out the drawers and dumped out all the papers she had in them. She spread the papers around, and found one card paper.

"Avonlea, what does this say?" Colomar picked it up, and showed it in front of Avonlea's face. Avonlea read it, and it had a nine- digit code.

"It's a code?"

"YES! I usually VC (video chat) with my family, but you're here! Type this into that box!" Said Colomar. Avonlea picked it from her.

"Alright." Avonlea left down stairs really quickly, and Colomar followed her and hovered next to her. Avonlea lifted up the card, and typed the code into a dial on the side of it. "1-5-6-5-2-5-3-8-9." On the screen of the dial, it said "accepted." The suit box then opened up automatically. Folding out onto the counter top, inside is a grey protective foam. In the middle are eight white stickers. A note is in the middle for Colomar. Colomar hovered over to the suit case confused.

"Huh?" She said.

"There's a note, hold on." Avonlea picked it up. "Dear Colomar Junlo. Hope you're doing good, and having someone read this to you. If you didn't mind, we made a minor upgrade with these neuro-leggings. Place one on each side on bare skin on both foot, middle of lower leg, and middle of thigh and middle of hip. Hope everything is going great, take care. From you friends at AIRA." Neuro leggings?" Said Avonlea. Avonlea turns towards where Colomar was at, but she was gone in an instant , along with the eight circles.

"OH, MY STARS!" shouted Colomar from upstairs. Avonlea turned towards the stairs, and heard footsteps that weren't hers. Avonlea getting really excited with a big smile on her face. Footsteps coming from the stairs, and coming down, stepped forth Colomar! Changed into a new outfit with a purple crop top, black shorts and bare feet. Colomar came walking up very proud, and with the biggest smile on her face, and so did Avonlea.

"Oh, my stars! I'm waaaaaAAA!!!!" Colomar lost her balanced and fell forward. Avonlea caught her, and stood her up, but Avonlea had her arms up for her to catch.

"Oh, my stars, Colomar! You're walking!" Said Avonlea.

"I KNOW!!!!" Colomar teared up with happiness and excitement. Dancing around, and stood still.

"I don't even know what I'm crying, I've walked before with my old enhancers!" Said Colomar. Colomar fell over, but Avonlea jumped to catch her.

"Woah, bud, take it slow," Avonlea laughed.

"Right." Colomar slowly got up, wobbling back and forth, and side to side. "Just, excited, I think?" Said Colomar. She walked around for a bit, and even jumped around Avonlea. Even did a little dance.

"Were these the leg enhancers you were talking about?" Asked Avonlea.

"What? No. My old ones were like….uh….skeleton- looking pants, but these are WAY better!" said Coloma, as she . continued to walk around. Avonlea was looking out into the darkness outside of her house with the tall grass waving, and the only source of light being the moon and the porch of Colomar's house.

"I better get going. I try sticking to a routine every night when going to bed," said Avonlea.

"Aw. Alright. Well…see ya," said Colomar as she stared at a figure which she thought she was Avonlea.

"Over here," said Avonlea. Colomar looked.

"Oh, hah," she said and waved bye at her. Avonlea slipped into her shoes by the door, opened the door and walked out of the house. She closed it right behind her to begin walking on the trail she took to get to her house. The view all around seemed magnificent as the tall grass waved in the moon light. The slender trees all around cast their shadows, and Avonlea was only able to see the silhouettes and headlines of the tree heads. She viewed the distance hills, and beyond that the moons, and the rings around Seighdarr. When looking into the deep part of the forest, it's pitch black.

Avonlea did begin to think about one thing when she took in the view. She stopped and looked back to the barely visible view of Colomar's house, but kept walking. She slowed down to and stared at the gravel ground, but spaced out.

"It's just the one. I got five more after that. After all, it would really help her. But she said....oh...never! She'll love it! Overwhelming of course..." Said Avonlea. Feeling mixed feeling in her chest, but then more exciting than the other feelings.

Not taking long for Avonlea to get back home, but she did have to go around town in the trees to get back to her ship. Just over a big head cottonwood trees, and in familiar grounds, Avonlea had gotten back. With a door on the side where the cargo bay is , Avonlea unlocked it. Just like a normal door she opened it up where a stair case came down and climbed inside into the bay. Lights automatically turned on. She turned around to close and lock the door behind her

"Phew....long day..." she said. Her ship has two built-in rooms, and they have two beds built into the wall. It's right next to the cargo bay where a hallway is at on the right side of the ship. The left side of the hallway is the two rooms and the right is the washroom. One large sliding door opened up when Avonlea walked out of the cargo bay, and into the hallway to head left into the sliding door of the washroom.

Later on, Avonlea came out in her pajamas , which are a big and baggy orange shirt and baggy blue shorts. She nicely folded her other outfit and set it next to the sink in the washroom. She closed the door behind her, and walked straight across to the room. The door slides, and lights automatically turning on as she entered. To her left are the two beds mounted on the wall, and on the right is a mounted in desk is a gamer office chair. Metal boxes stacked on top of the desk, and more on the upper bed. Also having boxes near the door in the corner and some in the middle and next to her bed. Some of them filled with her personal items, and other things. Her own black and blue backpack on her bed. Coming over to her bed, she zipped it open to take out a velvet red handbag. Opening it up, and a cyan blue glow illumined from it. Looking in she smiled to close it back up.

"Yeah, she'll love it." She places it back in her backpack and zips it up. Picked it up and set her bag next to her bed. Lifting the covers, and sliding into her bed. Light switches next to her bed, and she flips them off to have her room pitch black. She got comfortable by turning and tossing to find that sweet spot on the bed. Finding it, she closed her eyes, and went to sleep.

The time scale on Seighdarr is a long longer than twenty-four hours each day. Since Seighdarr is bigger than five earth suns that were in a single line, the planet's turning radius takes a lot longer. The minutes, hours, days, weeks, months, and years are all longer on

Seighdarr. Instead of sixty seconds in one minute, it one-hundred seconds. Along with minutes, it's one-hundred minutes in one hour. Days are fifty hours a day. Weeks have fifteen days. Months have nine weeks in each one, and twenty-five months in one year. Let's do a little math here. In a single week, there are fifteen days, and nine weeks in one month, so there are one-hundred thirty-five days in one moth. What about in a year? well...there are three-thousand seventy-five days in one year. That's ten times the amount of days we have. Surly they have a lot of time, since they age slower than other beings do. The average Kausnian, but Avonlea is race called an "Ocnian," but similar, needs the same amount of sleep of seven hours, but still have a lot of time during the day and night. Some people on Seigh-darr don't need to sleep naturally, but Avonlea on the other hand, and Colomar do.

From the time it was yesterday, which was 40:00 L.D. (Later day,) to 17:00 E.D. (Early Day.) A total of thirty-seven hours from when Avonlea slept to early day the very next day. Turns out that Avonlea didn't immediately go to sleep last night, but watch on her phone her favorite shows on the internet, yet it did take her the thirty hours. How wise her time was spent, but sleeping the rest of the sev-en hours until the dawn of light the next morning.

The air is cool with a small breeze blowing through the trees. Her ship stood in the light, and all electronics shut off still on her ship, but a power gauge mounted in the wall began to blink a flashing red. Not beeping, but blinking towards Avonlea's direction. She's a heavy sleeper, and it didn't faze her at all, but she's so used to getting up early in the morning, her body got used to it. Naturally, Avonlea began to wake up, and the red light began to show in the pitch blackness. She slowly cracked open her eyes, and seeing the bright light. She blindly felt around for the light switches to find it, and turn on the lights. She saw the gauge on the wall, and a small message next to it saying "Power Supply: Low."

Closing her eyes and dropping her head, Avonlea removed her covers from her bed. Legs out first, she stood out of bed. Hair all messy, stretching her arms she walked barefoot on the cold metal ground to walk over to the room door where her cat sippers are at. She slipped into them, and walked over to the gauge to press a button.

Yawn, "ugh.....gotta......recharge the ship," she said. Rubbing her eyes, the door to the room slides open and walks out. The ship powered by electric the ship is eco- friendly. Avonlea walked down the hallway where she went left into another hallway. Two more rooms are in the ship and at the very end of the hallway is the control center to get the ship up and going. Walked by the first room is the small kitchen area. Then walking by the second room which is a small computer room. Offer to the control center which has four seats. Two in the very front and two just behind the other two with controls. The main pilot seat is on the second row on the left. The main window to view the outside is big as a bus windshield. Avonlea walked over to the pilot seat, pressed a couple of buttons and switches to turn activate the solar panels that flip open on top of the ship.

She heard the humming of the panels flipping open, the ship began to charge with the gauge she looked at. It doesn't take long for the ship to get a full battery as the percentage was at seven percent, and now is at twenty-six.

"Hmm...food or get ready first? eh...to get it out of the way, get ready first," she said. She walked back down the hallway to pass the computer room and kitchen. Turning right where the rooms are at on the left, but the washroom on the right. The sliding door to the washroom slides open for Avonlea to enter. Getting ready as like anyone where she brushes her teeth, bathes, puts on the same cloths she left by the sink, and folded her pajamas' to put by the sink. She walked out with her yellow goggles all steamed up, and her hair still damp. Feeling really hungry, she goes to the kitchen room where the door slides open. The kitchen is really small, and is also slip into three sections. When she entered, she stood next to a small dining table with four chairs at each side. One side is the cooking area with a stove, cabinets and microwave mounted into the wall. Then two more cabinets on the right, but it took up the whole wall. The top one has food, and the bottom has three water jugs. The water jugs are for a water dispenser with half a jug of water already asserted in. It makes a total of four jugs of water she has.

Going to the small cabinets to get a red tea kettle, walked over to the water dispenser to fill it up with water. Going back to the stove, she turned it on and waited for it to boil. Going to another cabinet to get out dishes. A yellow bowl with a smiling face on it, and a whale mug with the whale's tail being the handle and the mouth have a space for one big cookie. She placed the items on the counter top, and went back in the cabinet to get a small brown box that had cream of wheat in, sugar, and cocoa container along with a cookie jar. Setting all the items down, she grabbed the brown box to pour cream of wheat into the yellow bowl. Grabbed the cocoa box and sugar box to put one teaspoon into her mug. Grabbed one raisin cookie out of it to put it in the mouth of the whale. She heard the whistling of the tea kettle. Walked over to turn it off, she grabbed the kettle and poured it into her yellow bowl and whale mug. Setting the kettle back on the stove.

She got a spoon and mixed the hot water and cream of wheat in the bowl for it to slowly puff up. It did, and she added a bit of sugar into the mix. She stirred it until it seemed right to her. When it did, she stirred the spoon into her whale mug until it mixed in. After that, she puts the spoon into a box for cleaning later as there is no sink in her ship. She looks back at the food she made and took a whiff of it. Mainly smelling the hot cocoa, she made.

"Hmmm," she said. Picked up her mug and bowl to take it in the computer room. When she entered the computer room, on the sides are seats, and desks all around, and in the middle is the main console. This console is the same size as the dining table, but longer in length. This console is used for showing holograms of maps, information of the universe, and information of species of animals, people, and planets. But, only one desk she went to which has three monitors. This desk is hers, and is well organized. The desks, the table itself, all are computer like two with holograms of screens appearing out of them as well. She placed her food on top where a hologram of a computer keyboard appeared. She swiped it away to make it disappear, sits in an office chair and kicked her feet up. She held her whale mug and dipped the raisin cookie in the hot cocoa and took a bite. Eating one half and dipping the other in the cocoa and raised it to her face to take another bite and to finish it off.

She then took a drink of her hot cocoa. Her body getting warm and felling so relaxed. "Aaaahhh....." She said. Taking two drinks of it and finishing the whole mug. She began to eat her sweet cream of wheat. After eating her breakfast when her bowl is halfway empty, Avonlea turns on the monitor, which by the way, doesn't have glass screens in the middle, it's just the metal frame of the computer, but it has a hologram screen that appears in all three monitors.

. But on the third monitor to the right had one message saying "Activity Reported on Seighdarr Atmosphere." She ignored it by deleting it.

"Sorry. I can't," she said. She changed the screen and put it to a video website where she could watch her favorite internet show.

Later, she finished up her breakfast, puts her finished bowl in the kitchen. She goes back to the main control to check on the batter percentage of the ship, and it was at one-thousand percent. The ship runs on ten batteries, but barely uses the power of each batter, so the power is slowly being used over time. It only takes a year for all the power to deplete. She pressed a button and the solar panels folded back into the ship.

"There," she said, "that should last me a life time." She went back into her room and packed her backpack to go out to visit Colomar. With her blue backpack, she already had that red velvet bag packed inside, but when browsing around her room, she found a green glowing bottle.

"Hm? What's this?" She said. She picked it up, and she knew it's a magical potion of some sort. It had no labels or any special indication of anything that it could have been a speed potion, strength potion, jump potion, or a flying potion. She knew it was just a bright green. "Eh, could be useful. I had it in my room, so it must be good for something," said Avonlea. She placed it in her bag, but insecurely. In a case of any emergency, she grabbed a small medical kit and three highly compressed water cans in case of fire. The cans being the size of a soda can, but held up to fifty gallons of water, and being super light as well. She thought of everything, so she zipped up her bag, stood up and swung it around her back to strap it on. Before leaving the room, she stood in front of the door and thought about if she really wanted to do what she is about to do with Colomar. In her conditions, Avonlea thought it would really help and she would be glad for her. She walked out of the room to go down the hallway to the side exit door, sliding open with the ramp extending downward to the tall grass.

Stepping down and closing the ramp and door behind her, she began running around town to find Colomar's house. The sun shone over the hill and barely at the tree heads to cast small shadows. She saw the town in the distance waking up with hover vehicles hitting the road. Running through the forest by the town, she passed by some normal runners who got their exercise every morning. Running and running by to get to Colomar's house, Avonlea went to run by a hill that lead into the forest with the tall and broad trees that stood everywhere. Finding the gravel path, Avonlea ran down it. Running and running, she eventually came across her house. Finding it with ease when there is light. The porch lights still on. She thought that she didn't know she turned on the lights at all.

She came up to the porch and walked up to the door. Checking the time with her phone to see it is 19:95 E.D. in the morning. Almost 20:00. Avonlea knocked on the door, and hearing faint footsteps approaching the door, and those steps getting louder and louder as she suspects Colomar approaching the door. Avonlea suspicions were true as Colomar came up and opened up the door wearing the same outfit from last night.

"Hey, how's it going, man?" Said Avonlea.

"I'm sorry, who am I looking at?" Said Colomar.

"Avonlea here. The one and only."

"Oh, hey, Avonlea. Come in," said Colomar, but in a very low-key way. Colomar slowly walked back to her dining table area, and sat down. Avonlea slipped out of her shoes and set them by the door. She closed the door behind her and walked in. The lights in her house were all off, and windows open with the sunlight shining through. Colomar had her phone collected to a wireless speaker to play her music. She sat there at her dining table and tapped her fingers. She didn't look as energetic as she had been yesterday. She didn't look like she wasn't having it at all today. Avonlea walked over and pulled up a chair and slowly scooted over towards her.

"So, uh...how's your morning been strollin'?" said Avonlea.

"Oh...it's morning?" said Colomar.

"Yeah, it's morning...why?"

"I didn't even know. I didn't sleep at all," said Colomar.

"What?!?!"

"I just been here ever since......and did some thinking. Alone with my thoughts." Avonlea scooted in closer.

"Alright. What are those thoughts?" Colomar rolled her eyes and snickered to say nothing. Avonlea scooted in even closer towards her.

"Come on. I take to people with weird thoughts like I have. Like I thought....are elves and dwarves the same? Or are dwarves just mini size people and elves are REALLY mini size people? Or…the other time when I thought about that why do they call comodo dragon the "comodo dragon?" If it doesn't have wings like a regular dragon…..?"

"It's…with me. I don't know what to do…..with myself. I know I said to you about all that about me being blind and said "it's for a reason," but I wish I could at least see for a whole year, or just see in general. Goes the same for walking. My enhancers….yeah, they help me walk….but I have limits with my old ones, and this one glitches out so often, and doesn't work at all. If I only could go back in time and tell my little self to be careful…" said Colomar, and laid her head against the table.

Avonlea energy went low, and watched her. She felt her energy left the room, and felt like everything went a little dark at that point, but everything being the same. Avonlea scooted closer to her.

"I'm so sorry, Colomar. I know it sucks and unfair…but…I've seen many people with other disabilities, and they also make it through and make their days as if they never got it in the first place…." Colomar flamed up and quickly turned towards her angrily.

"Don't!——"

"I know! I know! I shouldn't be comparing you to other people, and you're not them. You're you, and I know that. I've also met some wonderful people who would of really like to either speak, walk, see, and others…." Colomar's flames went away and she turned away, but with the same mad expression. Avonlea turned towards her backpack on the floor, unzipped her backpack and reached in, but the lighting was poor, so she couldn't see what she was reaching for. The only thing she could see is the green potion she had packed, but noticed she felt something wet. She reached into that potion bottle an brought it out. The twistable lid that was on it had popped off, and was no all over her hands, and the bottle now being half full.

"Uh-oh..." said Avonlea. Colomar turns towards her.

"What?" Said Colomar.

"I just.....uh.....I have a magic potion, but it has no label, so I don't know what it does. I could do anything....." The potion covered her hand, and made holding the bottle slipper and it began to decline out of her hand.

"WOAH!" Avonlea said and tried catching it with her left hand, but it slipped out of it, and caught it with her right hand, but slipped to drop it on Colomar. The potion then poured on the back of her right shoulder.

Colomar couldn't see the potion, but felt it, and she got a little mad about it.

"Oh....my stars....I'm sorry, Colomar. Let me just....." Avonlea touched her shoulder with the potion on it....but that's when a bright light shone from it, and all Avonlea saw was being blinded from the light. Avonlea had closed her eyes, but slowly opened them up and rubbed her eyes.

"Ugh....what potion was....that...?" Avonlea looked around, and noticed the tone of her voice changed. Not into a different sounding voice, but a familiar voice. Avonlea looked around, she couldn't see anything, but outlines of things.

"Oh-no..." said Avonlea. She turned right, and saw the outline of someone standing next to her.

"Buena pena...what happened?" Said Colomar, but in Avonlea's voice. For the two had switched bodies. Avonlea realized something, and quickly said...

"Wait! I remember what this potion was! It was.....uh.....we switched voices!" She shouted in Colomar's voice.

"Switched voices?" Said Colomar in Avonlea's voice. Colomar in Avonlea's body rubbed her eyes.

"Yeah...but don't open your eyes!"

"Why? I can't see anyways."

"It's...uh....if you do, or I do, or either of us do, this will stay permanent!" Said Avonlea.

"Okay. You know about this more than me, so what do we do?" Said Colomar. Avonlea couldn't see, and from Colomar's eye sight, she only saw the outlines of things. Even looking outside, she saw the outlines of the grass, but no colours or anything beyond that. Looking at her own body, she saw a silhouette of herself, but that was it. Avonlea knew a decision she really wanted to make. Avonlea felt her shoulder still wet. Not able to see the potion, but with a drop of it on her fingers.

"Here, I got some on my hand. Touch it, and we'll switch back!" Said Avonlea. Colomar reached right.

"No, I'm on your right now."

"Why?"

"Because I'd be closer." Colomar went with it, and touched her hand. Evening blinded her Colomar's sight, the light still shone and blinded the two. Avonlea rubbed her eyes to open them. Being back in her own body, she looked around and was able to see everything. She looked to Colomar, and she looked around.

"Did it work?" Said Colomar, and she noticed her own voice.

"Yeah, it worked." Said Avonlea.

"Wait, why are you to my left now?"

"I just sat back in my chair. Chair is comfortable." Avonlea quickly looked to her backpack, and reached in to feel around. eventually, she felt the velvet bag moving around. She grabbed it, and pulled it out to set on the table. She opened it up. Avonlea took in a deep breath and let it out.

"Alright.......Colomar."

"What?"

"I know....it sucks being like this. Even with these enhancers, you still want to walk, or run even and be able to see. Believe it or not, I can make you walk, and may be able give you the chance to see." Colomar wasn't excited, and thought what she was saying was rubbish.

"I'm serious!" Avonlea reached into her velvet bag, and pulled out a glowing turquoise stone that's the size of a quarter. "I can heal you...with this!" She said. Colomar turned to see the silhouette of the stone, but not the glow.

"What is it?" Said Colomar.

"This....is a Turquoise Healing Stone. It has the power to heal anything. If you lose a limb, this can get it back!" Said Avonlea.

"Pfff...I already tried potions and other types of magic. Nothing works, Avonlea."

"Oh, but this is universal magic. It works for anything! It's just....do you want it?" Said Avonlea. Colomar didn't think it will work at all, or think it could do it.

"Eh...whatever. Try it," said Colomar.

"YES!" Said Avonlea. Avonlea had to do a ritual by closing her eyes, crushing the stone in her hands, and once she opened it up, the stone hand turned into a lotion type substance that glowed a bright cyan. She rubbed her palms together for them to glow bright. Avonlea opened her eyes where her eyes were glowing bright cyan, too. Closing her hand, and holding out her index and middle finger, Avonlea rubbed a piece of the stone across her forehead, poked her thighs, lower legs and feet. Avonlea closed her eyes, and put her palms together and said "Náyííłdzíí'." She opened up her eyes to see the stone potion sink into her skin, and all the glowing faded away.

Colomar looked at herself, and still had her same vision.

"Told you. Thanks….." suddenly, Colomar's veins glowed a bright cyan, along with her legs and eyes glowing. Colomar felt a great energy course through her. That's when her eyes began to sting out of nowhere and her legs started cramping up.

"Ow! maldición!" Shouted Colomar. Avonlea on the other hand had the biggest smile on her face, and had both hands into a fist and held them against her chin. Colomar rubbed her eyes, and slowly began to open them. The light shining bright. The view from where she was sitting showed the grass waving in the breeze. Avonlea stared at her. Colomar squinting, but she slowly made her eyes incredibly large! Staring at Avonlea with her eyes, and leaned closer.

"Avonlea?" Avonlea chuckles.

"Hi, Colomar." Colomar slowly tilts her head down, and held her hands up to her face. Seeing the lines on her palm. She then flamed her hand. Seeing how beautiful the flame is. Extinguishing it later. Colomar looked back at Avonlea. Seeing her eyes, nose, mouth. Skin colour, eye colour, hair colour, cloths.

"Avonlea. You're so...pretty!" Said Colomar, and tears began to form. Avonlea smiled, and also tears up. Colomar looked down at her legs, and slowly picked off the enhancers on her thighs, lower legs and feet to throw them to the side. She slowly began to stand up, without the enhancers.

"Avonlea..." Colomar said with her voice all choked up. She crying with tears of joy, "it worked!" She said, and covered her mouth. Avonlea began tearing up, too, and stood up. Colomar walked up to her, and they both gave each other the greatest hug.

Chapter 04:
Aloryn

"...that's the grass. That's the trees, the hills, the sky along with clouds, and beyond that is the universe with the billons of planets and stars," said Avonlea. Walking through the forest, they strolled along their own path, both Avonlea and Colomar. Slow and steady they went. They walked through the tall grass, and walking down a slope that had a ten- degree slope. It led to more trees, and in different types, and different colours. Colomar slowly walking, and stumbling as she walked. Wearing a totally different outfit with her wearing a green and blue tank top, and black shorts with green sneakers.

"Take it easy. Your body has never used your leg muscles, so you need to take it easy. In about two days, you'll be able..." that's when she fell over.

"Woooooaaaooh!" Said Colomar, and fell. Avonlea held out her hand. Colomar didn't take it. "It's fine, I got it," said Colomar, and slowly got back up to wobble around. Avonlea held her hands out in case she fell, but Colomar was able to balance. "I just can't believe it!" Said Colomar, "oh, my stars! Everything is....! I don't have words for it!" Avonlea laughed.

"I know you would be. I was kind of scared how you would handle it. Leaning towards overwhelmed, which you are, but you're handling it very well. Or you wouldn't like it at all."

"Why wouldn't I like this? I LOVE THIS!"

"Trust me, I healed someone with those stones, and the person hated me for it. I don't know why, but he did."

"Oh yeah! What did you use to heal my eyes?"

"Oh," Avonlea reached into her backpack to pull out that velvet bag, and opened it up to pick one of the turquoise stones. It glowed bright in her hands.

"I already said, but this is a Turquoise Healing Stone. Able to heal anything." Colomar stared at it as it glowed.

"Woah! That is so...pretty!" Said Colomar.

"I know. They're super rare, and only found in space. I only had six of them, now I'm down to five." Colomar stopped, which made Avonlea stop, too.

"You used one of this, for me?"

"Yeah, of course. Everybody in the world needs the gift of sight! And able to run through fields. I'm not sure how your life was going to turn out if I didn't heal you, but your life will be going up from here."

"I don't know what to say?! How can I thank you?!?!"

"Hah, yup, but you don't need to repay me. All I ask is you to be my friend," said Avonlea.

"Yeah...well duh! I just don't to do next? What will my friends, family and the doctors say?!" Said Colomar, and yellow flames admitted from her hair. Avonlea sets her hand on her shoulder.

"Well....I don't know exactly, but I'd take it slow. You're seeing everything for the first time. I go in order from telling my family first. Mainly my parents. Telling my friends and then my doctors.

Tell them that a friendly Astranaut came by and helped out by....well, healing you."

"Astronaut?"

"No, an AstrAnaut. Not an AstrOnaunt."

"What the heck is that?"

"Let's just say that I used to be part of a group called the "Astrals", a Universal Task Force, and are biggest thing is helping everything in the universe," said Avonlea.

"Huh. Alright," said Colomar. She started walking again, but stopped.

"I'm thinking of going back," said Colomar. Avonlea turned around.

"Oh, really?"

"Yeah. I'm overwhelmed by everything! I'm still trying to put things together, or...I DON'T KNOW! I never seen an actual person in my life! And seeing someone with eyes , mouth and....well....anything! I have to tell someone! My family!"

"I get it. It's hard to really comprehend it all after......say... how long have you been blind?"

"Since birth."

"And how old are you?"

"Eighteen."

"Hey, I'm a year older. Eighteen years, you've been blind. Seeing the world for the first time. Well....remember that potion I spilled on you?"

"The voice changing?"

"It wasn't a voice changing," nervously said Avonlea, "It was a body.....switching potion."

"What."

"Yeah....sorry."

"It's alright, but why hide it?"

"Oh. Okay. Not the reaction I'd expect."

"We switched back, and we're fine, dude."

"Well. Alright." Colomar began to lift from the ground.

"See ya later, Avonlea, and thanks again."

"Yup. Are you going to be alright?"

"Yeah.....yeah, I'll be fine. See ya," said Colomar.

"Oh, wait!" Shouted Avonlea, Colomar stopped, and Colomar came to her. Avonlea pulled from her backpack a sticky note, and a pen. She quickly wrote down her number.

"Here, call me if you can." Colomar took it.

"Thanks....uh.....I've never seen numbers or letters in my life, but....ill figure it out," said Colomar, "Well, see ya later," and flew away in the direction of her house.

"See ya, bud," said Avonlea, and saw her fly away and disappear in the distance. Avonlea felt great at that moment. Then, she ran off into one grassy direction, and thought about going to visit the town of Farmington, but lay low if the police could be looking for her from the other day. She ran over the hill and is at the edge of town. Looking to see people in the distance wandering about in the morning.

Running to the edge of town through the trees, she stood on the edge where a sidewalk crossed her path. She stepped onto the sidewalk and proceeded left. The couple of stores and shops along with some restaurants in the town she saw, she seemed to be on the side of the town as every building she looked she saw the side of it. It seemed that the town was split into three sections. Avonlea walked past all of the shops to where a road is built next to the end of the line of the shops, and next to it is grass, and next to that is a wide river that flowed through the town. She saw some people in small boats with little sails. She saw some people who are half Kausnian and half fish. These people are called Tóyan's, who are just like mermaids. She saw one of the Tóyan's that had short hair, dark red skin, and his tail scales colour pattern looked like a hotrod car design of black with red flames on it. Swimming away from her, she saw some other Tóyan's swimming along, too. Not all Tóyan's look like a mermaid. Some look like a regular person, but with some fish aspects, such as the person's entire body has fish scales instead of regular skin. The scale would be either blue or a green with them having webbed hands and feet, along with gills.

She didn't say anything towards them, but saw her reflection in the water when crossing the bridge that goes right over the river. Another section of the town is the middle part, which is just a massive part with sport fields in it, a big playground, and lots of cottonwood trees. She looked at the third section of the town, and it's the housing area for everyone, and a very small area it is with only two rows of houses. The houses didn't look anything special with all of them from her view being the rectangular shape she's always seen, so she went right towards the park.

Hover vehicles stopped near it, but only three of them she saw. The pathway was made up of cement and sapphire as some of the bits of the path glared in the sun. I should mention that on this planet gemstones aren't rare at all. Worthless in other words. They are just as valuable as sand, rocks you'll find outside, or the grass.

Sure, sand and grass have purposes, for sand it can be turned into glass for windows, mirror, and other useful things. Grass is used for feeding the animals, or whomever can eat grass. Gemstones on this world is used just like sand, and they add cement for more durability.

. It's for people who have super strength or are able to break stone with ease. Such as Avonlea, but even if she were to turn her arms into jackhammers, she wouldn't be able to break the ground if she wanted to.

Anyways, Avonlea walked into the park and entered near a wide- open field with goals at each end. The goals for each end are for a game called "Punto." A soccer like game where the field is in an oval shape, and the goals are hovering five feet off the ground and move from side to side. The field is very shaded by the trees, and as Avonlea walked by, she saw someone in the middle of the field. Kicking an icosahedron ball, which is a ball with flat sides on the ball, instead of being round. The ball also hovers seven inches off the ground. The person kicked the ball around, and punted the ball into the goal. The person would go back to get the ball and kick the ball to the other side and hit a goal. The one person has pearl white skin, short royal blue hair and eyes, royal blue polo shirt, black shorts and royal blue and white knee- high shoes. She also had on royal blue bracelets on both wrists, a white headband and white belt. The person is the same person Avonlea met when she first came here, but doesn't remember her name.

The girl punted the ball, but Avonlea quickly ran towards the ball, blocked it to kick it to the other goal. She makes it, and yells...

"PUNTO!" the girl eyes light up.

"AVONLEA!" Said the girl.

"Hey, what's up....uh.....I'm sorry, I forgot your name, what was it? Nisha?" The ball came floating back towards the girl. She bends down to pick it up in her arms.

"My name is NASIA. We met exactly one-day, eighteen hours and thirty-two minutes ago."

"Dang, I don't even keep track of time. I watch the sky for time, but sheesh, you're persistant on timing," said Avonlea.

"I can always keep try of time with my n-new processors, I'm always connected to the internet and keep track of time in any zone." Avonlea confused.

"What are you talking? What processors?" Said Avonlea.

"I'm am a Cosmic-bot, so I have recently installed the newest processor that's up to date."

"Uh....a Cosmic-bot?" Said Avonlea, "is that what you are?"

"It's what I am, along with the billions of others all over Seighdarr," said NASIA.

(Robot people? That's cool!) thought Avonlea.

"Oh...I feel like a jerk now. I just moved here to Seighdarr from a different galaxy. I came from the Lyra Galaxy where....I guess there was never any Comic-bots?"

"Oh. That's alluring. Hmmm, from knowledge I just now gathered, there is no Comic-bots ever recorded in that galaxy," said NASIA.

"Yeah. But, whatcha doin'?"

"Oh, uh....I've been playing Punto."

"By yourself?"

"Seems that way."

"Hmmm...got any pals? Mates? Buds?" Avonlea asked.

"No. I don't have any friends," said NASIA.

"Aww...then I'm your first," said Avonlea.

"Really?"

"Yeah. I make friends along my journey. So...what do you like doing?" Said Avonlea. NASIA's eyes turned into the loading logo. Coming back with results.

"I like gardening, taking photos of lovely views, knitting, rubbish picking, and trying out Punto."

"How's that turning out?"

"Hmm...not as fun as I thought it was going to be," said NASIA, and drops the ball, and kicks a little.

"Well, it's nice to try everything. I tried all sports and hated it all. I tried them again, and I loved them all of a sudden. "

"What do you do?"

"I like going on adventures back where I was from. I love making, breaking stuff, and make friends and go sight- seeing along the way. Although, I don't know what there is to see around here."

"Oooh! There is a grassy valley around called Animas. There's a bridge that goes over the valley, and I've always wanted to take pictures!" Said NASIA. I've been trying to see it, but with up-updates, I haven't to."

"Oh, then how to you feel now?"

"All updates are completed as A1Z. 75. So, I won't be able to update for the l-longest time."

"So...wanna check it out? See some places? I haven't seen this place, I don't even know what part of the planet we are. And I've been attacked for the past time I've been here!" Said Avonlea.

"Certainly."

"Great, need anything? I got stuff here in my bag, just in case."

"Nope. I'm all set."

"Alright. You've seen it, so do you know where it is?" Asked Avonlea. NASIA's head did a disturbing spin around two times, which is kind of unexpected, but something Avonlea hasn't seen. NASIA's turned towards a direction away from Avonlea, and pointed.

"It is in this direction," said NASIA, and began walking. Avonlea followed her, just right behind her.

Taking off, and getting out of the town, which didn't take very long, the two began walking in the forest area that surrounded the small town. As the two were discussing, Avonlea discovered the name to the forests all around the town, and the one by Colomar's house. The cottonwood tree forests are called Animas Forest, and the one by Colomar's house is called Kiwanis. Following NASIA through the forest, she noticed how strange she walks. It's not like an average person's walk, but more of a robotic person- like walk.

"You've been here longer than me, so what is it like here?"

"Wrong, I've been here for two and a half weeks in Farmington. But it is true, I've been living here on Seighdarr my whole operating time. I love It here. It quiet, nice people, and I hear from conversation that some people come here to see the views," said NASIA, and NASIA's right eye extended out from her head and was turned into a camera. With a flash from her left eye, she began taking pictures.

"Whoa, I forgot to ask, NASIA, what are your powers?" NASIA turned to Avonlea.

"Oh! I am a shapeshifter, in a sort. I can turn into any electronic device. I mainly turn my arms and eyes into camera, clippers, holograph screens."

"Wait, what? so....you're like me?!" asked Avonlea

"Hm?" Wondered NASIA. Avonlea transformed her right arm into a chainsaw, then into a blaster, then into a paddle ball.

"Wonderful! I did not know that! Are you made of an Astrite material, too?" Avonlea turned her arm back to normal.

"No. I'm made of something called *Novo*. It's a skin and diamond- like stuff? I don't know, and I can turn into all sorts of things." Avonlea began showing off her powers by turning into a motorcycle, rubbish bin, a small tree, a tree and back into herself.

"Delightful. I can only turn into objects powered by electricity. If you don't know, I was created by my mother and father, Jaylün & Kyryn Yuna. My name is actually an acronym for Nanotech Artificial Sentient Intelligent Android."

"Huh, that's cool. So, you're living on your own, now?"

"Certainly. A good exercise, my parents told me that everyday my brain gains more information by living everyday."

"Nice," said Avonlea. NASIA began taking more and more pictures of tree, and some flowers they walked by. They walked by some flowers that are tall as them, and the   petals are like massive rings. They have a green stem, and light blue petals. These flowers with the ring pedals produce a bubble- like sap, and air would pass through them and form bubbles. These are called *Bubble Blossoms*.

"What about you? Ms. Avonlea? Where did you move from?" NAISA asked.

"Uh..." Avonlea said with hesitation, "I'm from....Kailaj."

"Kailaj. A planet in the Whirlpool Galaxy, and is five thousand lightyears from the pinwheel galaxy. You traveled long and far."

"Yeah. It was a journey."

"I bet your parents are proud of you for making on the long journey."

"Very!" NASIA began taking more and more pictures as she goes along. Avonlea just watched her, and watched their surroundings, as you don't know what could be lurking around. NAISA turns her arm into big hedge clippers and began clipping away pieces of a big bush that was in their way, and going through it. Avonlea stepped over the bush debris, and just behind those lines of bushes was the bridge that NAISA talked about. They had made it to a grassy canyon that split the area of Farmington to the other side of the land, and the bridge is an old brick viaduct that had bricks that were missing and broken off. It was covered in moss, vines and other plant life. Down below was tall blue grass with tall pine trees. The pine trees had green wooden logs and red leaves. Six- legged wild horses roamed around down below, eating the grass. On the other side of the viaduct was green plains of purple grass, and hills of it with no trees in sight.

NASIA began crossing the bridge without being careful.

"Look! It's just on the other side!" She said. Avonlea was not caring for being careful, too. It didn't matter if they weren't careful or not, besides the holes on the viaduct, since they are both lightweight. NASIA ran to the middle of the bridge and bent down to take a couple of photos. After taking five of them, she kept on walking. Avonlea came up to the middle of the viaduct, and saw the fantastic view of the canyon and more forests covering the land, and the hills over on the horizon.

She took in a deep breath with her nose, and let it out through her mouth. Turning left to keep up walking with NASIA, who made it over to the other side. NASIA was on the ground, and took photos up close of the purple grass. Avonlea walked up right behind her, and NASIA didn't notice at first, but there is a wooden sign mounted next to the entrance, but covered in vines and moss. The only reason she saw it was the light wood she noticed underneath.

"Orsio Plains," Avonlea read on the sign. NASIA stood up in amazement when she spotted something over in the distance.

"Oooh! Do you see that!?!" She said, as she points to look over at Avonlea. Avonlea walked over, and looked to where she was pointing. In the distance, Avonlea eyes lit up when she spotted a small herd of seven dinosaurs. These dinosaurs aren't unheard of to us, but these dinosaurs are one of the long necked dinosaurs, but this one is even bigger than the Argentinosaurus: the biggest dinosaur we've ever know. This dinosaur is called a "Emensiousaurus." So large and tall, its foot is as long as two school buses. Its body is bigger than the humpback whale, it's as tall as a football field, and its body is covered with a thick hard skin, almost diamond -like, but they have plant life growing all over them, with small animals living on their backs.

Avonlea and NASIA were amazed by all seven of them.

"Woah!" Said Avonlea, "let's get up close!" She said. Avonlea began running towards their direction.

"Wait, Avonlea," said NASIA, but she didn't listen. NASIA ran right behind her. Avonlea being quick, she outran NASIA who only had the one ability to transform. NASIA did quickly learn that she was able to transform her legs into hover shoes and quickly skat-

ed right after Avonlea. Avonlea ran up to the colossal animals, and
their footsteps shook the ground. They're so gentle while doing it,
too.

"Whoa! Kyrie wouldn't believe this! Hah hah!" Said Avonlea.
They also had a baby with them, and the baby are the size of two
brontosauruses .

"Aww!" Said Avonlea. NASIA ran up behind her, and
changed her legs back to normal. NASIA quickly took some photos
and changed her eye back to normal.

"These creatures are magnificent, but Avonlea, they can be
aggressive," said NASIA. Avonlea looked at her.

"Aggressive?" What do you mean by "Aggressive?" That's
when the mother noticed them, and her back began glowing a bright
blue.

"Uh....does it so happen that they....uh...?

"Fire lasers from their backs?"

"Yeah."

"Unfortunately, they do," said NASIA.

"Then we should....." Avonlea and NASIA slowly began to
walk, but that's when a large blue laser beam fired at them! NASIA
turned her feet into hover shoes, and Avonlea began to run for the
hills.

"Fasten our seat belts!" She said, and they both ran away
from the enormous beasts. They quickly charged up the hill, but the
mother has persistant aiming, and fired a beam at NASIA. Avonlea
was able to turn her right forearm into a translucent shield, but it
knocked Avonlea and NASIA over the hills. Roughly landing on the
other side and rolling on their sides. Slowing up, Avonlea got up from

the momentum of her sliding, and NASIA slowly slid over to Avonlea. Avonlea picked her up and stood her straight up.

"You good?" Avonlea asked.

"Untouched! Pictures turned out perfect so far!" She cheerfully said. With a hologram screen she turned her eye into projectors to show her the pictures she'd taken. Some were great, others not so much.

"My storage is up to one terabyte in store, but I have twenty-five-thousand-five-hundred-eighty-five terabytes of storage left. NASIA arose from the ground.

"Jeez, what do you do with the pictures?"

"At my home, I have a separate computer where I connect my memory unit, and upload all my-my-my-my-my photos." Then she gave a weird face when looking at Avonlea.

"Hm, are you sure all of your updates were done? You sound like you still have issues you ought to patch."

"A-A-A-Av-A-A-A-Av-Avon-A-A-A..." NASIA said, but began to glitch out, her eyes began to glitch out, too.

"Are you alright?" Said Avonlea, and waved her hand in front of her face, and snapped her fingers. It didn't work, so she moved her a bit.

"AAAWWWwwwwwWWWAAAAAhhhh!" She snapped out from it, "A-Avonlea, sorry, my reaction time is in need, but look! What is that?" Said NASIA, and pointed over shoulder. Avonlea looked into the distance. On the tall purple grass in the distance, something moving, but staying in the same position. She saw bright red spikes in the distance.

"I don't know," she replied. She turned her hand into binoculars, and looked through them, but only saw the red spikes, and they were moving up and down slowly. It looked like a breathing motion.

"Uh-oh," Said Avonlea, "come on." Avonlea began running, with NASIA following right behind her. Going up to the red spikes, Avonlea slowed down when she got closer to it, and was very cautious. NASIA stood close to Avonlea, and Avonlea turned her right forearm into a shield. She went around whatever it was, and it had a tail, and at the end of the tail were six red spikes. Avonlea put her shield away when she realized it was a Stegosaurus on its side. Avonlea put away her shield, and went to the front of the Stegosaur. It was barely breathing, and Avonlea walked over to the head to find it had its eyes closed. She bent down near the head, and checked it. NASIA then used a scanner built in her eyes, and scanned the Stegosaur.

"Nothing physically is wrong with the Stegosaur. Everything is fine, and this male Stego is at a young age."

"How did you spot that? Some physical scanner stuff?"

"Nero scanner to be correct. But I do not know what is wrong with this Stegosaur," said NASIA.

"What the heck?!" Said Avonlea. Avonlea snatched a bunch of grass and tried feeding it. It didn't take it, and looked away, and nodded off. NASIA thought of something, and a small satellite formed on her head. It spun around, and NASIA pulled up a hologram screen of her area, and around her area, there are twenty more life forms. All not moving.

"Avonlea, there are twenty......recalculating.......twenty-one lifeforms in this area. All of them aren't mobile."

"What the heck is going on?" Said Avonlea, she stood up. "Wait, you said, "twenty-one"?"

"Certainly."

"Where's that one?"

"It's located on my left, twenty-five-hundred feet away from us. It seems to be the only being moving."

"It must be making that Stego, and the other nineteen others feel the same way. Ugh! I'm sorry, this went from nice and taking pictures like a tourist to you and I being detectives of a murder mystery. Except our....uh....victims? Are still alive...............I hope."

"It is alright. I have one-terabyte full of storage, so I'm am enjoying my journey, so far, with you!" said NASIA.

"Aww, I'm glad to give you a spectacular one!" Said Avonlea, "Whomever eis doing this, might be able to do it to us, too. Could be some creature, a witch! Or.....I don't know. Whatever they are, I wanna help these animals. Do you?"

"I'm created to help anyone! Yes! I will be more than happy to help!" Said NASIA.

"Alright, thanks, we gotta move then," said Avonlea, "but be stealthy as you can possibly, flipping can," Avonlea began to whisper in mid- sentence.

"Alright," whispered NASIA. Beginning to lay low to the ground to hide them in the grass. Even though the grass is a grape purple, and NASIA and Avonlea have snow white and bright sky-blue skin. They both sneaked around in the grass, and with the scanners that NASIA had pulled up on her hands, they were getting closer and closer to the one mobile thing just behind a couple of large ruby gemstone growing from the ground. Closer and closer they were getting. Once getting close enough to where they think the thing is at, they sat right behind the Ruby. That's when the two suddenly felt the ground shake, and some dinosaurs, and other animals came running away from whatever chased them off.

"NASIA," Avonlea whispered, "I think it's behind this ruby. Stay quiet, and I'll check it out." NASIA nodded her head. Avonlea sitting in the grass, she slowly goes to check just right behind the ruby. Once she did, she saw a figure taller than they were. It was definitely someone, but she couldn't tell. She saw a Woolly Bison on its side, and a blue beam was emitting from its stomach. The beam also seemed to trail off just behind the bison. The beam followed that someone, and the person showed her face towards Avonlea. She immediately recognized the person, who was a woman three years older than Avonlea. Avonlea's eyes dilated, and her heart began to pump faster and faster. The woman has white shaven short hair, dark purple skin, yellow coloured eyes, and her lips are black, and she wore a translucent glowing blue, cylinder backpack. She wore a one- piece body suit with strange designs, and colours being dark blue and black, and a strange insignia on her chest and shoulders.

Avonlea turns towards to NASIA.

"OKAY! We gotta go!" Avonlea whispered.

"Why? What is it?" Asked NASIA.

"It's....someone I knew of, and she's incredibly dangerous! That's Annix Vivyzo!"

"I thought you wanted to help."

"I do! But I can't go up against her! She's strong! Her super power is she steals your energy until you don't have energy to breath!

I'll be taking your charge, for you!" NASIA was conflicted on the inside, and wanted to help.

"NO!" She said out loud, "I refuse! These poor animals need our help!"

"It's fine! They get there energy back, but she could...." That's when a green laser beam fired at them, and blasted off a big chunk of the ruby they sat near. Avonlea jumped into out of the open, and NASIA jumped behind the blown off ruby chunk. Avonlea's face in full clear view.

"Ms, Jyuinz. A pleasure to.....*encounter* you again," said Annix. Avonlea got up from the ground very slowly, and with a scared look on face, she turned around.

"Uh-uh-uh....." She gasped for air, as if it felt like something was choking her. "Nice to....see you to....Anni." Annix had her arms behind her back, and slowly walking up to Avonlea, with Avonlea frozen up. NASIA watched from the distance.

"I have to ask, how in the lightyears did you find me?"

"Oh....hah-hah, I didn't find you. This is a coincid~" Annix laughed.

"Oh, don't be silly, I knew you were here."

"What? How?

"Your Astral suit. Once activated, your Astral signal pulled on the radar. I just *had* to visit."

"Hah....well, I can't say I wasn't surprised to see you. I mean, this is great, seeing how~" Annix cut of Avonlea.

"How life has been after the fall of Azuna. I'd image it would be difficult. Well, you're still here."

"Yeah..." Avonlea said, and tilted her head down.

"You know, Vonyx can help you. I can help you. After every-thing that went down, I can't even imagine how your health is men-tally." Avonlea looked up to her, angrily.

"Never. One day, I'll all fall, then~" Annix quickly got up in Avonlea's face.

"Fall? By whom? If you're suggesting yourself, I doubt you'd do much without your precious star lost in space.

(Sigh) "You're right." Annix backed off.

"Hm. Great meeting you, after a while. But if you don't mind, I was already occupied with a task on hand," said Annix, and began taking the energy out from the Bison. Avonlea felt so furious on the inside, but scared is what she really felt. She turned away, and began walking towards town. NASIA, slowly got up, and walked alongside her.

"Avonlea, aren't we suppose to~"

"Look, they'll be fine. I'll just take a while for them to feel normal." Avonlea stopped, "Actually, I think of calling it a day. I have to do something for tomorrow. Early in the morning."

"Wait...but...."

"But....it can wait. See ya," said Avonlea, and she ran off from NASIA. NASIA watched as she left her, and looked back at Annix. Finished taking the energy from the Bison and moved on to another animal. She felt something inside her, something negative growing. As for Avonlea, she ran straight back to her space ship, from the pur-ple plains to the viaduct, to the forest and near the town, and then to her ship. She quickly opened up the side door and ran inside.

Once she got to her ship, she closed the door behind her with the lights turning on automatically, but right after, she angrily threw her backpack to the corner end of the hallway. She took in a deep breath and let it out. She ran down the hallway to turn left. Past by the kitchen and computer room to get to the control center. She jumped in her seat, and ignited three keys.

"I hate to admit it, but she's right. But I wouldn't call it...."lost." Oh-no. It's just playing a game of hide and seek. And it's been on a roll for five years."

Chapter 05: Bright Void

Walking pacing back and forth near the control console, she had an idea in mind that she doesn't know if she should put into motion. In her head, she began listing pros and cons about the situation beforehand .

"Alright...ALRIGHT! um....for cons.....uh....there's all the Onyx coming to me once they know I have a star. They could bring the WHOLE FLIPPING TEAM! I'll get in trouble with USTF, Arsenal, The CoPro's, Galatie, or Planetwatch. Or even worse....the flipping king of the planets. I rather be in a room of balloons than see him." She paced to the other side of the room. "Pros of this, I can use the power of the star to get them away from me. Hmm? I could take down one of the Onyx bases. I've seen the schematics of it. If they try to come here, Oh-hooo, they wouldn't stand a chance against me. Something I can go against to take down Annex. I mean, I have before, and I know where exactly where that star is........(gasp).....yeah!" She said. That's when she ran straight to her room, and quickly got changed into a suit. Not the suit she's wore before, no, she took out her pocket book, and set it on her bed.

She stepped out of the room once the door slides open, she had a new one-piece suit. It's black and white with a helmet unit in her right arm. The same suit when she came here, and now is leaving the same way. The suit is all white on the inside, but on the outside of it is black with armor on upper and lower back, chest, below the chest on her navel area, her shoulder, biceps, forearms, thighs, lower legs, tops of her hands and the top of her foot. She puts the helmet unit piece on. The helmet is a piece that goes around her neck, and the view side is a bubble- like helmet, but once put on, the viewing part air tightens around Avonlea's head and is able to breath regular oxygen. Right now, she's not using her suit's oxygen, but a vent through her oxygen pack opened up on her ship, so she'll breath the oxygen that is already present.

After she puts on the suit, she goes to the control center, and got in her seat. The ship has already been activated and the rocket booster began to whir, hum, and hover jets beneath the ship fired up. When she got ready with everything, she began pressing buttons and flipping switches. The hover boosters began to press against the ground, and the ship began to take off, and hover over the grass. The trees around her blew against the force of the engines. Leaves flew out, and making them fly above the ship's head. The ship began to hover over five feet, then seven, then ten. In order to not be noticed Avonlea activated a cloaking device. It doesn't make her ship invisible, but it turns the ship into a sky blue colour with clouds on the bottom, so I'll appear as if she was in the sky.

This ship is meant to be operated by four pilots, but being the only one, it took longer for her to steer, accelerate, or even take off. She began setting coordinates in the ships mapping system, and where she wants to go is seven galaxies away from where she is now. So, she angled her ship towards the sky, and accelerated the ship towards the sky at a quick speed.

We all know that our planet has five atmospheres. The troposphere, stratosphere, mesosphere, thermosphere, and exosphere.

But the planet Seighdarr has twenty-seven atmospheres. But thanks to Avonlea placing in the coordinates, and finding the location where Avonlea wants to be , she set the ship to autopilot, her ship is equipped with a lightyear-drive. A mechanism on her ship that allows her ship to travel above the speed of light. Her ship began to make noises as she began to reach the first atmosphere, Avonlea looked at a monitor, to see that small town.

"Well....I made good friends. Oh...Colomar's life is going to improve from a hundred to a thousand percent. NASIA was a cool friend for my last day, which I didn't know was my last day. But, I'll see 'em again one day. I promise." The ship then began its lightyear-jump, and in a microsecond, her ship took off to the void of space!

Galaxies she traveled. Going outside of the Pinwheel Galaxy, to travel several galaxies away from Seighdarr. She flew by stars, asteroids, rubbish left by other rocket ships, other planets, other suns, other galaxies. So vast in the unknown universe. That's where her ship spotted a dark yellow galaxy. She flew into it at unimaginable speeds. Once Avonlea knew she was in the galaxy she wanted to be in, she quickly stopped her ship from going too fast. The ship is able to maneuver through small asteroids and other space debris. But this galaxy she entered had too many asteroids to move around in, and she ship was unable to dodge them all, so she manually began to fly the ship herself. Asteroids everywhere she turned. The ship is equipped with ion cannons, and able to blast through the asteroids, but only the small ones. The big asteroids, when she blasted them, wouldn't break, but only break off the top layer . She accidentally fired, and some of the asteroid debris would come fly at her. Thankfully, due to her piloting skills, she maneuvered through them. In the distance, far from her, there is another white sun, and in the other direction is a large planet size asteroid.

Avonlea landed the Hyper Nova on a very large asteroid the size of Mount Everest. The ship, still having its cloaker on, it blended in with the rock. She turned off the ship, and the gravity immediately went away, and she floated out from her seat.

"Whoa! ha-hah!" She laughed. The ship had magnetic landing gear, so it stuck to the side of the ship. She switched her breathing from her ship to her suit air tank, and the air tank is a little pack on her back. It's small, about the size of a notebook, but her suit is able to turn the carbon dioxide back into oxygen. She jumped around in her ship, and floated near the back of the ship to the hallway near her room. The door in the corner was the entrance to her cargo bay, and is the only way to get outside. She opened up the door, and floated into the cargo bay. Before going out, she made sure she had shut the door, and locked it. She floated to the controls to the left of her, and she pulled the lever to open the cargo bay door. Lights began to flicker, and warning sirens sounded off.

The air in the cargo bay got sucked out, and she was pulled towards it, but it only happened for a second. The door slowly opened up with the insides camouflaging to blend in with the rockyness outside. From her view, she saw asteroids floating around, and beyond that are the stars, and beyond that is the black void of space, with the sun shining to her right.

In her space suit, she was able to use her transforming powers, so she turned her right arm into grappling hooks. She shot the cable at the rock outside, and pulled herself towards it, and floated around. She saw a specific shaped asteroid in the distance.

"There it is!" She said. She turned her left arm so it can blast a grappling hook, and began shooting herself towards that one asteroid. Suddenly, her helmet showed her she got an incoming call from an unknown. "Oh stars...I swear to flipping gosh! If this the phonicars again, I'm flipping my sweet honey ice tea," she answered the call.

"Hello?" A familiar voice said.

"Hello? Who's this?" Said Avonlea.

"This is Colomar. Is this Avonlea?"

"Oh scrap. Colomar. Hey, how's it going?"

"Oh, mis estrellas, Avonlea, it's been....great! I just finished the world's longest video chat with my whole entire family." Avonlea reeled herself towards a small asteroid.

"Dude, how did that go~?"

"My family was ecstatic about it. My mom passed out, and my aunt exploded. Literally!"

"Hah hah! That's great."

"I told them everything, and now they're all coming to my house."

"Oh....for...?"

"They wanna celebrate. Like....my whole family."

"Oh, scrap man. Party hard."

"They also ask if you could come. Since you healed me?"

"Uh.....hm....I....uh....I think I can come? For a quick visit."

"Not for the whole thing?"

"Well...maybe. You just caught me doing something really important."

"Oh, I'm~" suddenly the call went static, and cut out to end.

"Huh. Call ended. Maybe it's the asteroid metal?" Said Avonlea. She tow- hooked herself closer and closer towards an asteroid. As she made her way, she thought about collecting an asteroid to store it in the cargo bay. The asteroids out here have a metal called "astrite." A metal two times stronger than titanium. Same element that NASIA is made of, too. Closer and closer she came floating around, when she came to the certain asteroid. The rock has five perfectly in-printed circles all in a single row. The asteroid she got near is a size of a semi-truck, so she floated around to the other side to find an X imprinted into the rock.

"X marks the spot," she smiled. She grappled onto the asteroid with her left arm, and transformed the half of her arm into a drill. She began spinning it, and drilled into the asteroid with debris flying at her. Extending her arm deeper and deeper into the rock, and trying to reach the center. She did when her drill head hit something that's not the asteroid, and transformed her arm back, and pulled it out. She looked within, to find a small black and blue truncated icosahedron container. She reached for it and pulled it towards her. "Oh, my stars, thank gosh! it's still here!" She said. Excitement overwhelmed her, and she began to open it up with all the sides of the container being a code. "Let's see....it is....A-V-O-N-L-E-A-I-S-T-H-E-N-U-M-B-E-R-1-A-N-D-S-H-E-R-O-C-K-S-T-H-E-U-N-I-V-E-R-S-E." The code worked, and the container bags to turn and split into two parts and slid open. Inside is a bright white light that shoneas bright as the sun. Avonlea turned a part of her head into a pair of sunglasses to look at it. Inside of the container is a white star crystal. It's not an actual star, no, stars are still large clouds of gas that turns into plasma.

This is a Uni-star. Stars that can power anything, and the big cities on any world are powered by these. These kinds of stars are super rare to find in the voids of space, especially the white star. They can come in all kinds of colours, and the colours all have purpose. If you were to find a blue star, they have good and positive energy, along with white, purple and green. Another star colour would be a yellow star, but these yellow ones are too wild to control, and sometimes can blow up with the crazy amount of energy they carry. Orange and red are negative energy, and cause bad effects, and if they are in hand, they burn as hot as the sun, and change their personality at random, or cause machines to go crazy, or overload to self-destruct. Even if they are close to machines, they cause these effects, and blow up if handled too carelessly. They could also just blow up randomly.

This white star Avonlea has is rare to find. Companies travel the universe to mine these stars and sell or power them in towns or cities. When they sell them, they are way too expensive. In the billions range if they were for sale in US dollars. Avonlea picked it up in hand, and these white ones don't burn in hand. Actually, stars are living beings. With all stars having their own personality, and being able to move on their own. They walk, but levitate, and can fly at the speed of light. The white, blue, purple and green all have personalities of any normal person. The yellow stars have a jumpy and ecstatic personality. Orange and red act angry constantly. Avonlea has a female star, that's she's always treated with respect, and kindness.

"Hi, Nizhoni. Miss me?" asked Avonlea, and hugged her. The star glowed even brighter. The white stars showed emotion by how bright they were. If they appear brighter than the sun, they are either excited or happy. If they shine just as bright as the sun, they have neutral feelings. If they dimmed down below that, they are either mad or frustrated. If they turn almost a dark grey, they are depressed. They can also refuse to give out their power if they want to. Luckily, Avonlea has been hiding Nizhoni all this time, and is very kind and polite.

"I'm sorry for leaving you there for five years, but listen, Nizhoni, bad people are on the rise once more. I need your help to put an end to it all." Nizhoni, turned a dark grey. Avonlea let go of Nizhoni, and white stars are able to levitate and float on their own. "Look, I know Azuna....blew up. But you and I can prevent another one from....well, blowing up, when we stop the Onyx." Nizhoni stayed dark grey, and floated lifeless. "Oh, stop it! Things will be bright. Just like you from now on. We don't have Kyrie or...the others with me, so it's just you and I. So please.....I need your help, Nizhoni. We'll make the universe a better place. One step at a time. Well you don't have legs, but...you get what I mean." Nizhoni then slowly floated towards Avonlea, and stayed the dark grey for a minute. Until she glowed a bright white light. Brighter than the sun!

"Hah-hah! yay!" Said Avonlea. Nizhoni floated towards Avonlea, and Avonlea made a circle on her chest. She made her chest open up like an aperture camera to reveal a small chamber she created. Nizhoni floated inside the chamber. Closer and closer she got, until she got inside, and Avonlea closed the chamber. She suddenly felt a jolt, and a surge of power coursed through her body. Making her eyes glow and her veins.

"WHOA!!! HAH-HAH!!! OH MY GOSH!!" She shouted. The power of the star powered Avonlea up. "Settle down, Nizhoni, it's been a while. Whoa! Five years is a while," she said. Just on a shadow from an asteroid, she saw a shadow quickly veer out of view. It wasn't like a slow asteroid moving around in space, but a shadow that suddenly just moved. Avonlea turned around, and looked around to find the sun in the distance, and the asteroid slowly floating around.

"Uh-oh." Suddenly, she saw the glare of an object come flying at her. She leaped out of the way of it, and three more of the objects came flying at her, but she grappled onto an asteroid to dodge them all. "Someone is definitely~" suddenly, a person with two neon green hook katanas came flying at Avonlea. Avonlea jumped to an-other asteroid, but saw the glowing green blade of the hook katana come charging at her. "Okay! Okay! Not this time! Not this time! NOT THIS TIME!" The katana came flying at her, but missed and was about to go over her right shoulder, until she caught the handle. "Oh, my stars! I caught it!" She shouted. The blade of this katana was an emerald green with ocean wave designs on the blade. A cut in the middle for a hook, a black hand guard, and a neon green handle with neon green cable attached to the end.

Beyond the glow of the blade, she saw another darting at her. Avonlea didn't take a chance of this one going through her, so she turned her arm into her blasters, and shot it before it hit it. The laser beam bade the flying blade turn into a different direction, and the blades were pulled back to the user. The user was standing on an asteroid. Staring at her with two yellow snake-like eyes.

"Dokubi," said Avonlea. Dokubi is someone Avonlea knows, but aren't fond of each other. Dokubi has neon green skin, wears a black suit with dark green armor on her chest, shoulders, back, arms and legs. She also has black colour lips, and she has a black cape with a hood. She has her hood on until she put it down to show her head with no hair. She held two neon green hook katana's, and at the end of the handle it was attached to a bright neon green cable, and the cables are attached to her forearm. She held them backwards, and leaped off the asteroid she was on, and threw them at the asteroid Avonlea was on, and pulled herself to get closer to Avonlea.

Avonlea turned her feet into magnets so she can stay on the side of the asteroid. Somehow , Dokubi did the same, and began walking towards Avonlea while she dragged the katanas, but floated around. It really surprised Avonlea that she wore no space suit at all, and was wearing what she always wore with her black suit and amour. With a device on Avonlea's suit, she activated a speaker so she can speak outside in space. Even though there's not sound in space, but with the technology Avonlea's suit has, she's able to speak to her, and Dokubi is able to hear Avonlea. Dokubi began to swing her swords in a circle. She held onto the chains and swung them over her head, and onto the ground. Cutting up the outer parts of the asteroid. Green sparks would come flying up, and vanish.

"Heeeeey, my ol' pal....Dokubi," said Avonlea, and wickedly snapped her fingers at her. Dokubi stared at Avonlea with her lifeless eyes. Dokubi didn't speak, and slowly came walking over to Avonlea, and Avonlea backed up. Sparks would fly at Avonlea. "I'm just confused how you're breaking the laws of physics here. How do you create sparks with your blades if there's no air?" She still didn't speak.

Dokubi threw her blades at Avonlea, and she ran across the asteroid, and super jumped off of it, and leaped to another asteroid. Avonlea ran and ran, and Dokubi threw her blades again. Avonlea jumped and did a back flip to changed her arms into blasters to fire at her. Dokubi deflected her blaster lasers back at her and missed. Avonlea stood on an asteroid, and changed her arms back. "Wait! Wait! Dokubi! Listen!" Avonlea shouted. Dokubi jumped towards her, and kicked her to the wall of the asteroid and had her foot on her chest. "Wait, listen. It doesn't have to be like this! We call be friends and sit on a hill to watch the ocean."

"You think you are saving anyone with this star? I've seen the future through fortune teller. Astral's the last one standing when Seighdarr falls," said Dokubi.

"Then you need to find a better fortune teller. I don't know what you're talking about," said Avonlea. Avonlea transformed the center of her chest into a star shape that lit up. It got brighter and brighter and blasted Dokubi with a beam of energy! She set Dokubi flying to another asteroid. Avonlea then turned her legs into rocket jets, and flew away as far as possible. Since there's no air in space, there's no wind resistance. She came to an asteroid, and hid around it. Dokubi was jumping from asteroid to asteroid trying to find her, but saw how useless it is. She pressed a device on her ear.

"Mission failed. Star is already inserted."

"It's fine. Phase two is already in progress. Return." Dokubi then left.

Avonlea flew around, and hid behind asteroids.

"I'm like you, Nizhoni. I'll become the world champ for hide and seek," said Avonlea. She flew around, but that's when she got a call from the same number from earlier, which was Colomar's number. "Oh, signal's back." Avonlea answered it, "Hey, Colomar, what's up? Sorry, I don't think I had any service out...."

"Hello," said an entirely different voice, but sounded familiar. Avonlea stopped her rocket boots, and floated around. "Who's this?" Said Avonlea in a concerning voice.

"I don't know. Maybe someone you know. Or the purple pal that you met at the plans."

"Annix?!"

"That's my name, don't wear it out."

"Annix!" Avonlea said with anger, "what did you do with my friend?"

"Which one? The fiery girl? Or the robot girl?"

"I swear, Annix, if you hurt them! So, help me!"

"Calm down. We're just....."contractors" for this town. Dokubi, Korai and I. Town seemed lovely, but in a great area with plenty of resources, I'll be a good base." Annix hung up.

"NO!" shouted Avonlea. Avonlea began to feel anger course through her. Her face began to turn purple. She jumped off the asteroid, and flew back to her ship once she found it. It was unattacked, luckily. She closed the cargo bay door, and with anger, she broke the door handle to the second cargo bay door and flew inside. She flew straight to her pilot seat, and quickly activated the ship. She set the coordinates, and the ships began its light speed trip to Seighdarr. Her ship is able to save each location she's visited, and since Avonlea put her space ship near the town, that's exactly where her ship is going back to. To Farmington. The rockets revved up, and her ship began flying in above the asteroids. The light-drive charged up, and the Hyper Nova blasted off and out of the galaxy!

Not knowing that there was a small red ship just right behind her, Avonlea traveled over the other galaxies again. Past all the planets, asteroids, and other people who travel the galaxies at a regular car speed. Her courses were set on the Pinwheel Galaxy, and her ship flew straight into it where she passed by nine other planets. Her ship stopped when she got near the planet of Seighdarr, and was around the rainbow rings. "Come on! Faster!!" She cried. Suddenly, her ship shook, and a lot of her stuff in the ship jumped around. She had been hit by something, and it continued. She looked back at a monitor, and there was a small scout ship tailing her, and blasting lasers at her rocket boosters. The ship had no shields, so the rocket boosters were taken down with ease. One out of four rockets blew up, along with the controls inside the ship, and other components. It sent her ship spinning out of control, but going in the same direction towards that small town.

Avonlea got thrown out of her seat, and went bouncing all over the controls. She wasn't able to jump back inside the pilot seat. It kept knocking her around the ship, until a metal crate came flying at her, and impacted her directly on her forehead. Things went blurry, and went dark.

Chapter 06:
Cinder and Ashes

Smoke burst out of pipes, shrapnel, and debris flew into Avonlea's face, as she lay on the corner in her ship. The controls broke,   lights were flickering red, and she felt nauseous. She got up, and the shrapnel and debris covered her body. The ground slanted, and angled to where couldn't walk on it. She got up, and stood along the wall.

"Ugh.....what happened?" Said Avonlea. That's when she heard a *BOOM* in the distance. "Oh-no!" She said. She immediately got up, and climbed up in her ruined ship. Some parts of her ship blew up, but she was able to miss it. She took off her helmet, and thought of changing into her other suit, so she turned her legs into rocket boots and flew into the room. Her stuff was scattered everywhere, with her pocketbook stuck by the doorway . She opened it up and picked it out. She took off her space suit and put on the suit that was stored in the coin. Activating the coin, the suit took over her entire body. The door to the cargo bay had the broken handle, but the door was also dented. She blasted it with her blaster, and entered the crooked cargo bay. The main cargo door had blown off, and saw the debris and destruction her ship had brought when crash landing. It turned out to be night time, and she saw a tree on fire, and ran back to her room in the ship.

Earlier, Avonlea had packed compacted water cans in her backpack. She saw her backpack on the right side when she entered, and dug through her bag to find the compacted cans. They were all unattached, and she loaded all three of them in her left arm. She loaded one of them in her right arm where she formed a water cannon. She then began to spray the trees that were on fire, and saw some animals run.

She heard more *booming* in the distance, but she couldn't recognize where she was. She flew up in the air, and saw nothing but the forest, although there were some trees on fire, which she flew to and quickly put out. Turing around, she saw the town in the distance, and saw the town with smoke exhausting from the town.

"No! I gotta~" a huge tree came flying at her, and she was hit out of the sky. The tree took her down and threw her on the ground. She slid on the ground, with the tree holding her down. Her left arm was caught, but the wood pierced through the water cans and water blew out of them. She only had the one, and she was using that arm to move the tree off of her. The ground began to shake, and she didn't know what that was. The ground exploded just a couple of feet from her right, and a figure jumped out the ground. It towered over her. Dust arose, and stepped forth a tall and muscular figure.

"Oh! Nice shot!"

"Wait? Vora? Was it?" Said Avonlea.

"IT'S TORA! TORA VIGORUS!" Said Tora. Tora had on the same coloured suit that Annix had worn.

"Tora, wait. You don't know what you're getting yourself into, here."

Tora stood tall, and her face glared at Avonlea. Attached to her for arms are astrite metal gauntlets. They are able to both turn into the hand gauntlet and a drill. Tora turned them from a drill to the hand.

"I know exactly what I'm going into. My new boss is paying a lot for me to be with them, and you know what they say....you pay for what you get," said Tora. Tora came charging at Avonlea. Avonlea blasted the tree off of her, and jumped into the air.

"I don't have t~" she was hit again in the air, but by something bright. She was thrown at Tora where Tora held her by the head and swung her to the ground to step away. The wound on Avonlea's head had already made her dizzy. The bright something that threw her came over to Avonlea. It was a red fire that burned so close to Avonlea. From the flame stepped forth a figure.

"Ugh..." said Avonlea, and moved a little, "Korai? Hey, blow-torch, how's it going."

"Argh! I HATE THAT NICKNAME!" Shouted Korai, and Korai blast fire from her palms at Avonlea, who quickly crawled out from the hole. Korai wore a black suit, like Dokubi's, but instead of green armor, its red with the aperture logo on her shoulders. Korai has a sky red skin colour, black and royal red coloured eyes, and has short royal red hair. If it ain't obvious, but she has fire powers. Avonlea blasted Korai with her water cannon, and sent her flying back. Jumped in Korai's way came Vyroz who blasted webbing at Avonlea. Vyroz missed, but Avonlea blaster her with her laser blasters.

"Argh! Vyroz!?! You too!?!?! But what do they offer that you don't already have?"

"Offered people. Vyroz consumes. Universe full life." Vyroz spun some webs at Avonlea, but she sliced through them with swords she made out of her arms. Tora came charging at her, but missed.

She watched out for Korai, but she saw a pair of wings take off into the night sky, and set fire to more trees. Korai also has the ability to change into a fiery red phoenix bird. She flew towards the town, drawing Avonlea's attention. Avonlea has her legs in jet mode, and flew off to leave Tora and Vyroz behind. Korai setting fire and fire-blasting trees, and blowing some others.

"KORAI! STOP!" Shouted Avonlea, and put some of the tree out with her water cannon. Korai changed form and flew towards Avonlea to grab her by the bicep. With a fire-blast from her palms, she sent Avonlea to go flying and straight towards the town. Avonlea braced for impact and turned her back into a shield to take the concert road.

"Ugh...." Opening her eyes, Avonlea rolled over once she saw twin green katana's come flying at her. She got up, and jumped over a swing from the blade, and leaped over the next. Just behind her stood Annix who blasted her with a laser beam and sent Avonlea flying at a broken vehicle. She hit it, and got right back up. Korai came flying with fire blasting from her palms, but Avonlea jumped over the vehicle. Annix, Dokubi and Korai all stood right across from Avonlea. Bound for Tora and Vyroz to come any minute.

Avonlea has her blasters red and loaded pointed at Annix who stood in the middle.

"What did you do to everyone here?"

"Relax. They're fine. Oh, I mean....we're just the villains of your story and killed all of them. Do you really think that would go well with my conscience?" Said Annix.

"What is it that you all really want? I feel like it isn't the town remolding scrap," said Avonlea.

"Ugh....what else?" Annix saw Tora and Vyroz quietly walk right behind Avonlea, prepared just like the other three without Avonlea noticing. Avonlea looked down at her chest to see the star logo.

"Oh...no-no-no-no-NO! This is my baby, Nizhoni."

"It's for the great Onyx, A."

"The moon buster? yeah, I don't think so. You want Nizhoni? Break the piñata," said Avonlea. She charged up her blaster.

"Okay." Annix's arm turned green, and a green glow went around Avonlea and Annix has a telekinesis powers, and pulled Avonlea towards her. Avonlea resisted, so Korai blaster her fire to send her flying at Tora. Tora's arms were ready to catch, but Avonlea slide under them.

"Wait! Listen, I've said this from time to time, but come on! Please! We don't have to do this! All the people getting hurt. Lives you're ruining lives. Can't you see the bigger picture?" Tora decided to throw the broken vehicle at Avonlea, but she blasted her way through, until they all came charging at her. Korai came flying around to fire-blast. Avonlea used a shield she made from her forearm. Vyroz spun some webs at her, and electrocuted Avonlea to be stunned for two seconds. It locked her body up, but is still able to move and blaster Vyroz in the face. Tora came with a flying fist towards Avonlea, but she caught it. Dokubi swung her chain katanas around her waist, and pulled her back to swing her around.

Dokubi swung her toward Annix where she blasted Avonlea on the back, but came firing back with a laser to the chest. Dokubi held her blades and swung them at Avonlea, but with shields, she was able to block her attacks. She wasn't able to hold all her swinging blades, but cuts parts of Avonlea off. Literally loosing bits of herself. With each hit, or blast, bits of her came off and fell to the ground. Bits that she can't get back.

Korai came flying in, and kicked her with a fiery foot on the right side of her face. She lost a majority of her right cheek, but it didn't matter to Avonlea. Using every tool, she could imagine from chainsaws, swords, blasters, rockets, shields and grappling hooks, she couldn't think of anything else. Left and right she was kicked across the face, or any other part of her body, or sliced or blasted by everyone else. Korai fire blasted, Tora curb stomped when Avonlea was on the ground, Vyroz electrocuted, Dokubi sliced up Avonlea's leg, and Annix blasted Avonlea to the other side of the road. Thirty-four feet away from them. She slid on the ground with burn marks on her body, along with cuts, dents, and her limbs missing a lot of bits of herself. Her ear was gone, along with her cheek.

All five of them came walking towards her. Annix getting a communication on an earpiece. She pressed it and heard someone speaking.

"This Annix. Come in." The person speaking to Annix. "Understood." She turned it off. "New orders. Admin wants us to return."

"What?!" said Tora, "We're nearly done!"

"Argue with Admin. Not me." Annix began to fly away. Others began to leave, too. Vyroz, Dokubi, and Korai. Tora looked to her side to see Avonlea. She switched her gauntlets to drills, and jumped to the ground to vanish and drilled away.

Avonlea looked up from the rubble, and saw them all leave. She began getting up, but all the hits and blasts had made her weak. Even with the energy of Nizhoni. She had to stand up, so she made herself stand up. Even with the amount of bits she's lost, and the beatings she took. Heavily breathing, and shaking.

"Ugh.....is.......that~" she looked, and saw totally different figure come flying down. The figure wore the same exact suit like Annix, except dark red, it's black. Wearing a helmet, and descending from the sky.

"Ugh...what are you? The boss battle? I got plenty of fire in me, still. So, let's get it on!" She said in a faint voice. The figure came floating down, and landed in the middle of the road. A couple of feet away from Avonlea. She wore a helmet that is all glass, but all black. "What are you? Are you one of Oscuro's lackeys?" Said Avonlea. The figure stepped forth. With a press of a button on the side of the figures helmet, the helmet went away. Showing her face.

"I never mention Oscuro, did I?" It felt like Avonlea's heart had been punched, and also a five-hundred- pound weight had been dropped. Avonlea's eyes dilated, and breathing increased. She recognized the figure who has brown colour skin, shaven white hair, and red coloured eyes with a diamond tattoo in the middle of her forehead.

"Jyuniper?" Avonlea said with a surprised expression.

"Hm...sup?" Jyuniper said with a grin on her face.

"No......no.......no-no-no-no-NO-NO!" Said Avonlea, and her face began to turn purple, and tears up in her eyes, "We we're meant to travel and save the universe together! Along with the others, and you become one of them?!?!" Avonlea said in fury.

"Pffff.....wake up, man. The universe didn't need us anymore, and spit us out. They tore apart us all. Look at Kyrie, Streanlo, Solar.

Alekzandrya and Bomblbi are long gone. Join us, Avonlea to build a better future. All from one step at~"

"NO! You're destroying lives! Building bases for your own personal and needless uses. Jyun....please....don't turn now! We can simply go back to the Hyper Nova, and restart!" Jyuniper slowly peered down.

"I'm long gone, AJ. Plans are in progression. Now, you can be a major help by handing over Nizhoni."

"Nizhoni only sees my friends who are like brothers sisters to me."

"Were sisters." Avonlea formed missiles from her arms, and launched nine of them at Jyuniper. Jyuniper braced herself, and they all blew up in her face. Lifting dust and debris from the road. Jyuniper still bracing, and expecting Avonlea to charge at her. Which is expected, and Avonlea came flying at Jyuniper with a big fist to punch her to the ground. She formed a rocket drill out of her left arm, and launched it at her head, but Jyuniper rolled out of the way, and flew behind to punch her to the ground. Avonlea watched her, and her eyes began to glow and large laser beams fired out of her eyes. Avonlea quickly made a shield, and blocked it. It didn't cover for over five seconds as it burned parts off of Avonlea off.

Avonlea jumped over the laser beam, and came flying at her with a big foot to the face. Jyuniper caught her, and threw her to the ground where she broke it! Avonlea was sitting on her back, Jyuniper set a foot on her chest and began punching her left and right on the face. More and more bits came off of her. Jyuniper lifted her out of the ground, and blasted Avonlea into a brick building. Jyuniper slowly walked up to her. Avonlea turned her right arm into a blaster, and non- stop kept firing at her. Jyuniper is able to take each blast, with Avonlea terrified, and kept blasting the closer and closer she got. Jyuniper fired up her fist, and punched her on the right side of the face, causing Avonlea to lose the entire right side of her face, along with her eye. She didn't have enough of herself to form anything else, so she turned her arm into a sword, and swung at her. Jyuniper caught it, picked a device that once was clamped onto Tora before, which was a power lock that can cancel the person's super powers, and clamped it onto her right bicep, and was unable to turn her into anything else.

Jyuniper then charged up her hand, and punched straight through Avonlea's navel. Avonlea struggling to move or breathe, Jyuniper came to face to face with Avonlea.

"It's been a run, AJ." Jyuniper charged up her other fist, and aimed it towards Avonlea's chest. Suddenly from behind Jyuniper, Jyuniper was blasted with laser beams. She looks back, and saw men and woman in armored uniforms on a hover craft that came flying in.

"Put the civilian down!" Said one of the armored men. The hover craft they rode in said "Arsenal." More vehicles with that same name showed up, but Jyuniper had other ideas, and began flying with Avonlea in her arms. Quickly up into the air. One of the Arsenal hover crafts had blasters built in, and shot Avonlea and Jyuniper. Avonlea came flying down from the sky, and quickly took off her suit, and she barely has enough energy for one more blast to her blaster. She loaded her coin into her blaster, and shot it far away from her. As far as possible. She looked down and saw the head of the tree. She closed her eyes, and everything went dark.

Chapter 07: Aspsilize

The light beamed into her face. The cool breeze blew through her face, and the open wounds of her insides. The light warmed her face, and she is able to see with her one eye. Her whole right side of her face was blown off. Her navel area has a hole. Her right arm is nearly gone along with her left.

"Ugh……Nizhoni?" Said Avonlea. She opened her chest, and saw the white light glow, and Nizhoni came flying out. Nizhoni saw Avonlea, but Avonlea just hugged her. "I'm alright. I'm still standing. Itll take a lot more than that, Nizhoni to hold me down. I'd feel better if you stay in me for a while." Nizhoni then flew back inside the chamber in her chest. The clamp that was placed by Jyuniper to cancel out Avonlea's power and ran out of power over time, so Avonlea was able to pop it off with ease.

"Phew..." Avonlea looked around, and saw was in the head of a cottonwood tree, and not far from the ground. She leaped down, but didn't land on her feet, but on her side. Her red tank top, shoes and dark blue shorts were all ripped up, but that was fine. With her open wounds and missing bits, Avonlea is able to make herself whole. How? well, she's able to move her bits around from her insides to the out. She hollowed her inside of her navel, her arms, and thighs to fill up all the holes of herself. Which she did, but she is now hollow. She has also repaired her whole face. The issues with this is that Avonlea doesn't have the same strength as before, or can't change into anything she wants now, and is a lot lighter. She also gets very hungry .

She looked off in the distance, and saw some of the Arsenal vehicles fly over her head. She quickly ran to the nearest tree log, and stood close to it, so they weren't able to see her. She heard footsteps coming in, and wasn't able to make blasters, but is able to fight again. Just behind a tree a couple of rocks stepped forth and there is NASIA and Colomar right behind her. Avonlea felt joy when laying her eyes on the two together.

"NASIA! Colomar!" Shouted Avonlea, and they both say her sitting on the ground.

"Avonlea!" They both said and ran towards her. Colomar slid on the grass and hugged Avonlea, with NAISA doing the same.

"Oh, my stars, I'm glad you two are doing so spectacularly," said Avonlea.

"Yes. It was quiet neuro racking," said NASIA.

"Sheesh, I got scared. For once. I saw that dude fly with you and drop you," said Colomar.

"Yeah....I'm.....fine....It takes a lot to take me down. Where were you? And everyone else?" Avonlea asked.

"They all gathered the people, and stored us all in a storage unit."

"They didn't lock it, so we just ran out," said Colomar.

"Phew! That's a major relief!" Said Avonlea.

"No-one injured, but town is in major disorder. Arsenal has been assigned to find who was the cause." Avonlea notice the scratches on her arm and shoulders.

"What happened to you?" NASIA clearly tried to hide it.

"I ran into...uh...leaves when I was leaving the plains."

"Leaves? Really? The lightest thing did that to you?"

"Hmm...maybe I tried simple reasoning with that lady who were, in your words, "Taking energy from animals.""

"I told you to leave!"

"I'm sorry, but I couldn't~"

"Hold on. It's fine. In your heart, you thought it was the right thing to do."

"Y-yes..."

" Then I understand, but leave this stuff to a pro Astral."

"Hey. You've talked about these "Astrals" before, Avonlea. What is it?" Asked Colomar.

"And why do you have relations with that energy lady?" Avonlea shrugged, and sighed.

"Well, knew I was going to be telling you sooner or later. I thought it would've been later and not sooner. Settle down, and let me explain everything." Colomar and NASIA got settled and saw in front of Avonlea.

"So.....the Astrals are a universal task force team. Defenders of the universe for a thousand years, we've been making the universe a better place from foes with different ideals. It was my dream to make the universe a better place. To save those who are in need, or to help those who can't defend themselves."

"Was"?" Said NAISA.

"Yeah. It was my dream. Over time, people across the universe began to think that we're the cause of these incidents. The Onyx, which are the people who just imprisoned you in the storage unit are high- powered people who are with the Onyx. The Onyx's

goals have always been to reform the planet for peaceful times. But
how they do it is to destroy everything, and rebuild from there. They
blow up moons, and the debris of the moon would come into orbit
and crash on the place they came from. The Astral base was located
on Planet Azuna." NASIA's eyes began to make the loading signs.

"Hmm, I detect no~"

"Hey! I'm telling the story! Anyways, Planet Azuna was my
home. Then....it blew up."

"What?"

"How?"

"No-one knows. Astrals were disbanded, and the UUG have
declared if any Astral activity is in progress it is considered illegal.
So...ever since my home world blew up, I've been searching for a new
home. My sister and I along with another one of my friends named
Streanlo."

"Where are they?" Asked NASIA.

"Well.....we had a BIG debate, which caused all three of us to
fall out. Oh...how I miss my sister."

"Dang, Avonlea. I'm so sorry to....hear," said Colomar.

"I'm sorry, too," said NASIA.

"It's fine. I'm fine. Hah, you know to the brighter side of
things, because......because....what would be the point of being sad
and being mopey and dopey. You get nowhere.......and......it's gotten
me this far....hah...." None of them said a word for a minute.

"I'm sorry for making things weird. It's just me..."

"No, you're fine," said Colomar.

"You are, wonderful, Avonlea. I'm glad to have you as a
friend," said NASIA.

"Me too," said Colomar.

"Hm, thanks. So, when is your party?" Asked Avonlea.

"It's later, at night. You don't have to come~"

"Naw, I'm coming. It'll be my relaxation. And I assume you two met?"

"Yeah, NASIA. She's a cool bot."

"Aww, Colomar. You're the hottest Kausnian for having fire powers."

"How did you find me out here?" Asked Avonlea

"NASIA used....uh..."

"I used radar to track you."

"Yeah, that's it. OH! By the way, don't go to town. I saw a wanted poster, and you are on it," said Colomar.

"Sheesh. Alright. Geez. Anyways, can she come, too?"

"Yeah, I already invited her." Avonlea stood up, and began walking.

"Great, I'll see you then," said Avonlea. The two sat up.

"See ya."

"Bye!"

Avonlea walked back to her wrecked ship far from the town. The power had gone away, and she walked through both cargo doors.

"I can always rebuild," she said, and a piece of metal fell upon her head. She goes in, and turns left, and left again to her bed room. All dark with the lights barely flickering. She goes to find her cloths scattered, and some ripped up. She goes to the drawers under her bed to be unopened, and the clothes inside are unattacked. She opened up another drawer with a long black velvet bag. She then laid in her bed with the one pillow, and ripped up blanket on the bed. Rolled herself up in the blanket and went to much needed sleep.

The amount of time she took to sleep took up the entire day. From morning to late evening. At this time, she began to wake up, and felt energized. She arose from her covers, and got up forgetting that her whole wrecked ship is slanted. But she didn't care now, but only cared about going to Colomar's party. With one of untacked drawers she had on her bed, she pulled it out, and in a fancy white box she pulled out, she opened to see an outfit she saved for fancy occasions.

Meanwhile at Colomar's house over by Kiwanis forest are a great number of Colomar's family who had come over to her house to see her. Most of them are overwhelmed, ecstatic, tearful and happy. The main feeling is positivity at this party, and plenty of food is being made and served here. Colomar had on a bright yellow dress with a yellow belt and her regular purple sneakers. NASIA had gotten here before the party started. She had been helping with some of her family members make food. Now the two are looking out for Avonlea.

"Do you see her with your tech-y stuff?" Asked Colomar to NASIA.

"Yes, I do detect something on my rad~" NASIA spotted her, and Colomar did, too. Just in the distance slowly came up Avonlea in a new attire. She walked up to the two.

"Hey, you two," said Avonlea.

"Hi, Avonlea. You look wonderful!"

"Yeah..." said Colomar.

"Aww. Thank you," said Avonlea. Avonlea wore white knee-high socks with bright red flats. A red dress with a white belt and blue trimming. White gloves, and she wore makeup, like royal blue lipstick. A white headband, and white gloves. Around her waist, Avonlea had that black velvet back with her, which Colomar noticed.

"What is that?" Said Colomar.

"It's...something for me afterwards," said Avonlea.

"Alright. Come-come!" Said Colomar, and dragged Avonlea to the center of her family.

"Hey, everyone, I would like you to meet my friend, Avonlea," she shouted. Everyone knew who she was and gathered around her. Everyone thanked her, and told her how kind of an act it is. later on, they had begun eating, laughing, dancing, partying. They had the times of their lives just enjoying themselves, and eating food dancing to music, but it became evening, and that time of the night to call it in. As for the small town, well, they have been repairing it ever the incident, and on the look- out for any Onyx or Astrals. The repairing process is quick with a usage of technology being able to literally spray broken roads and fix it in an instance.

Avonlea sat by her house, and away from the party area. She sat down and watch the tree moons circle by overhead , and the rainbow rings. Eventually NASIA came walking over and sat next to her.

"This was a lovely party? Was it?" She smiled.

"It sure was." Colomar came walking over, and sat next to them.

"Avonlea, I don't think I can ever stop thanking you, so thank you."

"Hah-hah, you're welcome. Dude, your mom made the best chicken enchiladas I've had....well....in the longest time!" Said Avonlea.

"I know! right?! She only makes them during celebrations."

"I grabbed one, and once I took the first bite, I immediately wanted another one, but they were all gone, and she made a flipping lot!" Said Avonlea.

"Yeah, that's the thing, once there's food with my family, you gotta eat as much as you want!" Said Colomar.

"I'll take note if you celebrate again," said Avonlea.

"I am unable to eat food. Only enjoyment I get out of it is scanning it, and storing the flavors in memory," said NASIA, "It sounds and looked very tasty."

"Oh....NASIA, bud, it was....(kissed fingers)....the flipping greatest!" Said Avonlea. "But thank YOU for the party."

"This was all you! And just to say, I feel great! I'm flipping overwhelmed by some of the things I've seen. Like....a rabbit?! and I figured out some of the letters. The letter A is like a pizza slice with a cut in the middle, and upside-down."

"Ha-ha, what a way to put it," said Avonlea.

"Just...thanks, Avonlea."

"Stop it....it's what I do. I love helping for what I can. I thank you two for being my friends after all this time."

"You're welcome," said Colomar.

"My absolute pleasure," said NASIA. The three of them all sat on the hill side near Colomar's house, and watched the three moons.

KARL J. JUNES

Chapter 08: Tune

Avonlea has said her goodbyes to NAISA and Colomar. A fantastic party it was. Avonlea had left while wearing the same attire. She has her black velvet bag with her. She walked way outside of town. It was at a field where she came to, and it was the highest hill she walked upon the very top of it. She stood on the top, and had the view of the forest, the town in the distance, the viaduct in far view, and the forest area where her ship had crashed down.

How much rebuilding she has to do much later on, but that is much later. She came up here to sit down, and play a lovely tune. Sitting on the grass, she pulled the velvet bag on her lap to open it up and pulled out a dark wooden flute. The flute has a bear carving on the top, and the front has a blue ribbon tied on it. She closed her eyes, and began playing the instrument. The sounds of the flute carried in the wind as played her lovely melody.

She reflected on what she wanted to do next. It seemed her heart was set on is to the right thing.

It seemed like she began playing her music, and plays it as if someone, maybe from a different part of the world, can hear Avonlea's lovely melody.

About

Karl J. Junes

"I've overcome some big obstacles to become a better son, brother and author. I deem to be an outgoing, spectacular, brilliant-minded and notorious person that loves life, cats and the passion to be a success in my wonderful life, three times fold. I've always dreamt of a universe, so I wrote it to share my strange and fantastic ideas along with thoughts and the different patterns on life for those seeking an adventure beyond the stars."